Also by Lori Taylor

LIS

HOLLY WILD: Bambo

Thank you times ten to my Team of editors, Marie and Lisa,
who help make my story make sense, and to
Sleeping Bear Dunes National Lakeshore for making
my artist-in-residence stay memorable.

This book is totally Michigan-made!

Library of Congress Cataloging-in-Publication Data
Taylor, Lori
Holly Wild (Book 2) : Let Sleeping Bear Dunes Lie—1st U.S. Edition
First Printing, July 2012
Second Printing, September, 2012
Summary: Ten-year old explorer, Holly Wild, travels with her Team to
Sleeping Bear Dunes National Lakeshore where she faces ghost bears, her
fearest of Wild fears, while trying to help solve the Park's latest water problem.

ISBN 978-0-615-65973-2
[1. Nature—fiction. 2. Great Lakes—fiction. 3. Water—fiction.
4. Science—fiction. 5. Invasive Species—fiction.]
Library of Congress Control Number: 2012911512

Published in the U.S.A., August, 2012
by Bear Track Press, Pinckney, MI
Printed in the U.S.A. by Malloy Inc., Ann Arbor, MI

www.loritaylorart.com

HOLLY WILD:
Let Sleeping Bear Dunes Lie

By
Lori Taylor

Bear Track Press
Pinckney, MI

Sleeping Bear Dunes National Lakeshore

1 HQ (Visitor Center)
2 Crouch Farm
3 Dune Climb
4 Pierce Stocking Drive
5 Sleeping Bear Point
6 North Manitou Island
7 South Manitou Island
8 Valley of the Giants
9 Pyramid Point
10 Empire Bluffs

Manitou Passage

Lake Michigan

Empire

N

I heard the breathing, the panting,
felt the hot moist breath on my cheek. My skin crawled, my
stomach churned, my freckles sizzled. Bear!
But not just any bear.
A really BIG bear, times ten!
I turned to look it in the face.
It was worse than I thought and definitely not what
I expected to see. I, Holly H. Wild, was about to be
attacked by an—

BEARS! TIMES THREE!

"—Orange gummy bear!" shrieked Sierra. I jerked awake to find not a bear but Sie, my best friend, plucking a sticky orange gummy snack out of my hair. "Hold still. There!" she said placing it in a napkin. "It was camouflaged in your hair."

My heart was still pounding from my dream. I don't know how long I'd slept, but the humming of the van's tires meant we were still on the road.

"Thanks." I felt my cheek, the one that had been pressed against the hot window, and pulled off another warm sticky gummy snack. This one was lime green and covered in fuzz.

"Tierra!" I groaned. Tierra, or "T", my other best friend and Sie's

1

twin, was always hungry and always snacking. "Your gummy zoo fruit snacks are all over me!"

"Yeah, they kinda flew all over the place when I opened the package. Sorry. I thought I got 'em all," T said, shrugging. She was fixing her ponytails when she spied a less hairy, red snack on my shoulder and squealed. "Cherry camel! I was looking for you, mister." She popped it into her mouth.

The Team, T and Sie and I, along with my Gram and Aunt Kitty and her dog, Hunter, were on our way to Sleeping Bear Dunes National Lakeshore in Empire, Michigan. It was our summer vacation and the trip should be fun, but going to a park named after a bear made me nervous. Not just any bear, either,

but the great mother bear, Misha-Makwa, of the famed Sleeping Bear legend.

Aunt Kitty, a biologist and naturalist—meaning she studies nature—told us that we're going to Sleeping Bear Dunes to help her park ranger friend with P.A.W.—Park Adoption Week. Whatever that was, it sounded cool. I always wanted a park in the family. We already had an island in the family—Beaver Island, the one some of my Wild relatives had come from and the one we had left just this morning.

The ranger had also mentioned to Aunt Kitty that the park was having water problems of the mysterious kind, which got us GeEKs excited. T and Sie and I are GeEKs, Geo-Explorer Kids. It's a club we formed. We explore stuff and sometimes poke gross things with a stick, like poop, and collect bones and stones. The twins were excited to hit the beach. And me, being a Wild explorer and all like my relatives, I was ready to solve another nature mystery. We were about to embark on a new mission in the biggest sandbox in the world, or at least in my Michigan world.

"How's it going girls?" hollered Gram from the front seat. "Want me to finish the story now, Holly?" I had drifted off after the first part of the Legend of the Sleeping Bear. A hot crowded van with no air conditioning, the drone of tires, plus Gram reading, equals a sleepy Holly. I picked a hairy lemon yellow gorilla snack off the seat and fed it to Aunt Kitty's drool machine basset hound behind me.

"…and the mother bear, Misha-Makwa, along with her twin

bear cubs, escaped the fires of Wisconsin by swimming across Lake Michigan," Gram yelled, reading from my book *Michigan Myths and Legends*.

"This is not your fairy tale three bears story," I said to Sie and T. "This is the mother bear and her twin cub's

legend. The Goldilocks story is a fairy tale, this one's true." Sie rolled her eyes at me.

"The small cubs tired and the mother crawled up on shore to watch for them and waited for them to join her," Gram continued, "but they never did. The Great Spirit took pity on the sad mother and raised up her drowned cubs as two islands and set them before her. From her perch high up on the shore she could watch over them

for the rest of her days."

"Poor mom." Sierra shook her head and polished her glasses.

"Poor cubs," Tierra sniffed and popped another fruit snack in her mouth. "I mean—they were twins, like us." T was emotional when it came to animals, especially baby animals.

"Poor shore!" I said. "Bear claws are long. I can almost see the mother bear ripping up grasses and biting and splintering birch trees, peeling off their bark like cheese sticks," I gulped. Sic moaned. T grabbed her growling belly. The mention of food does that to her.

"Today, the islands are known as the North and South Manitou islands," Gram finished and slammed the book shut. Everyone in the van got all quiet except for the panting and snuffling of a hungry Hunter.

"And the mother still waits for them atop her dune. Asleep." I said smiling, successfully concluding the Sleeping Bear legend. I gazed out the window at the rows and rows of fruit trees in the orchards as we zipped by.

We left Beaver Island this morning, taking the two-hour boat ride back to the mainland's docks in Charlevoix.

Then Mom and Boy, my brother, drove Aunt Kitty's car back home with Kenny, my pet snake, and Wilma, T's hamster, and her babies. After our goodbyes, Aunt Kitty and Gram loaded the rest of us in our rickety van for the journey to Empire. And after all of the Hunter breaks, nature breaks, roadside stand cherry breaks, and Gram breaks, what should've been a two-hour van ride turned into four. So Gram decided to read to us to take our minds off our sweaty, smelly trip.

"Asleep. The mother still waits for them atop her dune

asleep. Today," I repeated loudly, mainly to comfort myself.

"Well, yes and no, Holly," Aunt Kitty piped in. There she goes again. Aunt Kitty, the well-meaning, nature-knowing naturalist, likes to put a hint of fright into nature facts. Kind of like how she adds a hint of peppermint or lavender in most things she cooks, to spice things up and keep us on our toes.

Even though my Team and I are GeEKs, we aren't totally fearless. I mean, sometimes exploring can be scary, that's what makes it fun. It can make you brave. But right now I would have been completely happy with a simple "Yes, Holly, she is still sleeping" response to my statement.

Things like spiders and snakes have never bothered me, but bears—it's a Wild family thing. My Wild women relatives were known for their run-ins with bruins or "bars" as my Great Aunt Daisy Crockett Wild called them. Ever since the day that she

Yooper cousin, Pauline

BeArs worried aBout us...

saved her brother Davy from one, and ever since Cousin Pauline Bunyan ran one out of her lumber camp and ever since Aunt Jenny Appleseed, famed for her Apple Brown Betty and Mountain High Apple Pies, was hunted across the Ohio Valley by bears, I knew my

Aunt Jenny Appleseed

...and we worried about BeARs!

time was coming. If it is my Wild fate to one day come face-to-face with *Ursus americanus*, a.k.a. the black bear, I hoped it wouldn't happen until I'm 25 or 30, really old and worn out. So the mere mention of non-sleeping bears makes me wiggly.

"But she's *sleeping*, right?" I asked again. Aunt Kitty giggled.

"Actually, she's still moving. Every year the dune erodes and gets smaller. Every day the winds and storms remove more of her sand."

"Oooh, Holly, the bear walks at midnight," Sie said, grinning, and making claw hands.

The thought of the dunes moving was disturbing. My stomach turned. Not at the loss of habitat or sand. But what would happen if Misha-Makwa were completely uncovered? Would she wake up? Would she stalk the dunes as a ghost bear? I didn't want to think about that.

"See that wooded dune over there? That's Alligator Hill," Gram shouted to us, pointing at a tall hill overlooking Sleeping Bear Bay.

7

"It looks like a giant monster reptile basking on the shore," Sie said.

"I had my fill of reptiles on Beaver Island, no offense to Kenny," said T. "I'm ready for good old-fashioned fun, and I'm ready to not see Ivy Buckthorn for the rest of the summer."

As we pulled into the Empire gas station I started to feel itchy, the kind of itchiness I get whenever Ivy Buckthorn, our archenemy, is around. After our run-in with the Buckthorns on Beaver Island, I hoped that by now she and her family were long gone. After bears, she is the biggest discomfort of my whole life. But I was sure the itchiness was because I was sticky and sweaty from the long, hot ride. I flicked a grape gummy fish from my new, old hand-me-down backpack and pulled out my bear bells.

"I'm ready for bear country now," Misha-Makwa," I said, clipping them to my belt. I wasn't taking any chances. None of us Wild women ever take chances—when it comes to bears.

LOST AND FOUND

After Gram picked up gas station groceries, we finally arrived at the park farmhouse. Standing large and white it looked like it came straight out of a storybook. Red barns, outbuildings, and a silo crouched next to it. Tall trees loomed over the yard, wide empty fields spread out in front, and behind it rose a dark, wooded hill. So, it was like an old, spooky storybook— one with bears.

Crouch Farm

"This is it kids, home for a week," said Gram, "compliments of the Park for doing volunteer work. Dinner after we unload the van, troops." We rolled out the van door, hungry for fresh air and food. Hunter was happy to be free and ran to visit each shrub, rock and tree. We hauled gear up the steps into the mudroom. Every time someone opened the porch door it squealed, then slammed shut behind them.

"We'll have to keep Hunter on a leash, too much wildlife trouble for him to get into," said Aunt Kitty as she tied him to a large picnic table in the backyard. I didn't think the table would stop him if he decided to chase a squirrel, but it could be an interesting ride.

I was lugging in my backpack, books and pillow when I tripped over something and fell flat on my face.

"OOF! Stupid rock," I said, rolling over to examine it. A

pink rock stared up at me, poking out of the grass. At first I thought it was one of Tierra's hair clips. But when I picked it up and turned it over in my hand it looked more like a large claw fossil or stone knife.

Holy creeps, my first Sleeping Bear Dune discovery! "I found a really cool artifact, guys!" I called. The Team, their hunger greater than their curiosity, stepped over and around me, dragging gear into the house.

"I can't believe it! I found it right out in the open!" I ran after them, following them up the steps.

"Believe it, Holly. You found lots of stuff on Beaver Island," grunted T, dropping her suitcase on the floor.

"And the last time you found something 'really cool', you had people screaming and climbing on tables," said Sie, unloading her camera and laptop bags onto a bed.

"But this looks like an actual artifact. The real deal." I showed them. It fit my palm just right. "It looks like a claw fossil, or a stone knife blade. Or maybe it's a knife blade made out of a big, fossilized, prehistoric animal claw," I said

"Maybe it belongs to Misha-Makwa. She is buried here, you know," said T.

"Holy creeps, what if you're right? A giant bear claw!" My jaw dropped. My guts bounced like a basketball. My freckles were sweating. The room got hotter. This must be what it feels like being terrified.

"Oh, brother, Holly. It's a stupid rock," said Sie. "Don't you think someone would have picked it up by now if it was an artifact?" She set her stuff on a bed along the back wall.

"Sometimes valuable things can be right out in the open. You just have to look to see them," I said.

"Or in your case, trip over them," said T, claiming the bed closest to the bathroom.

"But bones turn to rock after a long time. That's how fossils are made. If it got covered by millions of tons of sand millions of years ago it would, and there is a lot of sand here, it could be a claw fossil!" I squeaked.

"Maybe it's a message from Misha-Makwa," T said, stacking her clothes on the bed. "Like a good luck claw."

It would be cool if it was a fossil and an artifact and a good luck charm, times three. My claw-tifact. Maybe it'll point me to clues while we're here investigating water problems in the Park. It is her home after all. Thinking that made me feel better.

"Maybe," said Sie, "Misha-Makwa is telling you that your head is full of rocks. Maybe she's telling you that you need to take it easy. It's vacation; school starts in another month and a half. We'll have to deal with Ivy Buckthorn and fifth graders. That's enough stress. So relax."

The thought of evil Ivy and our run-in with her on Beaver Island made my freckles quiver.

"Dinner!" Gram called from outside. The twins bolted out

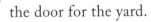

the door for the yard.

I slipped the rock into my pillowcase and followed the twins out the door.

POSSUM PICNIC

"It's a possum dinner tonight girls!" laughed Gram. "Possums eat darn near everything, and that's what we have!"

The picnic table was covered with leftover snacks from the trip and the groceries we had picked up at the gas station. There were day-old bagels, rainbow-colored ice cream sprinkles that looked like they'd been around since before I was born, a half a box of stale graham crackers, a bag of smashed M&Ms from the van, a bag of corn chips and a can of spray cheese.

I reached for a bag of hot dog buns, a jar of peanut butter and a banana. "PBB!—peanut butter and banana sandwiches. And with a slice of bologna it's a PBBB!" I yelled.

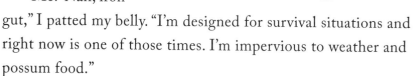

"Watch it, Holly, eat too many of those and you'll be up all night," warned Sie.

"Me? Nah, iron gut," I patted my belly. "I'm designed for survival situations and right now is one of those times. I'm impervious to weather and possum food."

"For dessert, a Traverse City cherry surprise," said Aunt

Kitty as she presented us with a bowl of fresh, bright red fruit.

"What's the surprise?" asked Sie, eyeing the bowl suspiciously. She was aware of Aunt Kitty's creative food efforts. They usually had some kind of weed or strange and unusual thing hiding in them.

"The surprise is I managed to hide them from Huntie on the way here!" Aunt Kitty joked, handing Hunter a bologna roll that he inhaled before it left her hand.

Sie sighed with relief and grabbed a handful and tasted one. "Not at all like gummy zoo fruit snacks. Much better!" she said with a squish.

"I hope we get to go to the beach tomorrow," said T.

"Oh, you will," smiled Aunt Kitty. "We're all going to help my friend Park Ranger Pearl with the Sleeping Bear Park Adoption Week."

"Yeah, what is that exactly, Aunt Kitty?" I asked.

"Well, volunteers and visitors get to help the park and have fun being citizen scientists."

I almost fell backwards off the picnic table bench. "Holy creeps! Really? That sounds awesome. What kind of stuff do we get to do?"

"There are all kinds of things to do, from picking up litter to measuring lake currents."

"Picking up garbage?" croaked Sie.

"Measuring? As in numbers?" I squeaked. Math was not my strong suit, that was T's area of expertise. I was more of a gross stuff, poop study kind of girl.

"What else?" asked T.

"Checking water clarity and taking water samples," Aunt Kitty said. "And it's not just picking up litter, but also sorting it, and taking notes on it to report on what was found."

"Organization! Collecting! Count us in!" We three cheered.

"Sounds like something for everyone," said Gram. The bowl moon appeared in a dark, velvet blue sky. Stars came out with cricket song. Just then a bubbling sort of whinnying sound came from nearby.

"Screech owls," said Gram. "Folks think they sound like wailing ghosts."

"How fitting, since the house is near a ghost forest," said Aunt Kitty. T and Sie and I looked at each other. G-ghosts?

"Time to call it a day. Tomorrow we have citizen science duties," snickered Aunt Kitty.

The owl cackled over T's head. She jumped and we all laughed. That's when an eerie laughter and yipping crackled over the field. We laughed again and the high-pitched yipping laughed back at us.

"Coyotes, answering their 'c-mail'," Aunt Kitty snickered at her joke. "That's how they communicate." We listened as they called each other.

As long as they didn't wake Misha-Makwa I didn't care.

FIRST NIGHT AT THE FARM

I grabbed my *Michigan Myths and Legends* book to read by flashlight in bed. The book flipped open to "…the mother bear clawed the shore, grieving for her children." My skin prickled with goose bumps. I closed the book and jingled my bear bells, then clicked off my flashlight and pulled my sleeping bag up over my nose.

"I thought you were excited to be here, Holly," Sie said.

"I am. But it's my thing with bears. I mean I'm not afraid of them or anything. It's just that we Wilds and bears go way back—it seems we all have run-ins with them sooner or later. We've had to protect ourselves and keep constant watch. Jenny Appleseed Wild lived in a cabin with saw blades across the windows to keep them from getting her. Cousin Pauline Bunyan kept a skillet near her bed. Even Gram has to be careful in the woods on nature calls." The twins snickered.

"It's not funny guys. The bells help warn bears that a Wild is in the area. Beaver Island didn't have bears. But here in Empire at Sleeping Bear Dunes National Lakeshore, well, it's all in the name." I clicked the flashlight back on just to check things out again.

"I'm just saying that since we're on their turf, in their homeland, or the mother bear's land, we need to be careful. All I can say is I hope the ghost bear is still sleeping." My stomach started to roil. Maybe my gut wasn't so ironclad after all.

"It's a story Holly. It happened long ago," Sie said, yawning.

"Remember what the storyteller, Charlie Bird, said back on Beaver Island? Some times stories are not just stories," I reminded the girls. "And just what the heck is a ghost forest anyway?" Creepy.

The girls were quiet. I tightened my grip on my flashlight. I could hear Hunter snoring in the kitchen next to the fridge. The clock on the tall dresser read 12:34.

It seemed I had just drifted off to sleep when something touched my head. I froze, not breathing. Then I saw something creeping towards me on the floor. I sat up and tried to focus on it. A glowing bear skull with gaping eyeholes and jaws grinned up at me.

"No!" I yelled.

"What's the matter? What happened?" T asked. Sie yawned, sat up and slid on her glasses.

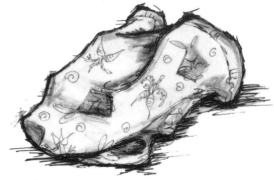

"It's on the floor, right there!" I gasped, pointing at the beast. Morning light peaked in through the slats of the shades, but the room was still dim. Sie got up to investigate.

"That's T's underwear," said Sie laughing. "They do look

quite dangerous. Especially with pink bunnies on them."

"It must've been a dream. I thought it was a bear skull." I was out of breath. I rubbed my head. It felt like I'd slept all night on a rock. "It seemed so real. I felt a paw on my head, then I saw a bear skull coming for me across the floor. That's when I woke up."

"Must have been your possum sandwiches," said T. "Those things would give anyone bad dreams."

As sunlight filled the room, the dream seemed silly. What a way to start the day. I was getting out of bed when my pink rock artifact fell on the floor.

"That's why my head is sore. I really did sleep on a rock." With all the nightmare commotion I forgot that I had put it in my pillowcase.

"Maybe that was your fated run in with a bear. Misha-Makwa's claw knocked your noggin and you survived," said Sie, rolling up her bag.

"Holy creeps! I think you might be right!" I yelped. Because it was a night-bear nightmare from a bear claw that bruised my head, then maybe I was home free! Maybe that was my big Wild bear run-in. What a relief. I would no longer be plagued with the Wild women curse. I could now focus on the park's water crisis. It was a good luck charm after all.

"Bring it on Mother Bear! Holly H. Wild is ready for action—but after breakfast." I was famished. I stuck my claw-tifact in my pocket as I ran to the door. "This could be Team Wild's biggest, wildest adventure yet," I said stumbling over T's underwear.

BEARS, GHOSTS & ALIENS? OH, MY!

We filed into the kitchen. Gram was flipping flapjacks. Hunter sat in the corner and caught pancake rejects that Gram tossed to him like Frisbees. Aunt Kitty looked up over her glasses from a book she was reading.

"Good morning, good morning, girls! We have a big day planned today at the beach," Aunt Kitty said, giggling and pouring maple syrup over a pile of pancakes. "Today we are doing battle with aliens."

T and Sie's eyes were as big as the hotcakes Gram flipped.

"Yep, we sure are," said Gram. She and Aunt Kitty seemed so unconcerned.

"Ghosts, aliens, and bears? What kid of place is this?" I asked. I couldn't believe my ears. Aunt Kitty seemed unbothered

by the fact that aliens could wipe us all out. I guess that is the calm, cool and collected way of thinking of the Wild women. I suppose if she didn't seem too worried then things were OK. And I guess if there were *real* aliens, she'd give them a

19

Pineapple-Lavender Upside-Down Salad. That's just the kind of person she is.

I grabbed a cup from the cupboard. "Do the aliens have anything to do with the mysterious water problem here?" I asked, filling my glass. Aliens must be stealing our water. I remembered Gram talking about flying objects and seeing lights over Lake Michigan when she was a kid on Beaver Island.

"Well, part of it, Holly," said Gram, smearing cream cheese and peanut butter on her hotcakes before smothering them in maple syrup.

"Some alien invaders arrived in the lakes over 20 years ago, and some even before then," Aunt Kitty said, shaking her head. "New ones are showing up in the lake and on the shore nearly every day. Not only can they travel by water, but by air, too."

Alien Slurp!

"Space ships?" asked T, gulping.

"Space ships? Oh, no, dear," said Aunt Kitty, "More like ore ships, or boats, actually. Ships are saltwater vessels. Boats travel the lakes."

"Aren't you worried?" I asked? "Shouldn't we tell the governor, the mayor, the townspeople?" I was amazed by their extreme calm. T and Sie stared, openmouthed.

"Oh, they all know, Holly," Gram sighed. Holy creeps times ten! I knew Aunt Kitty needed our help, but I didn't know it was going to be this dangerous.

"Some of these aliens have mouths full of teeth and voracious appetites. Others have long barbed tails and one big eyeball," said Aunt Kitty. I took a big swig from my cup.

"Gross," whispered T.

"Cool," murmured Sie.

"Alien invaders are everywhere," said Aunt Kitty, "but mostly in the water." I spewed my drink out across the sink.

"Holly!" laughed Gram, "What in the world's the matter?"

"Aliens! In the water?" I looked in my glass. I remembered Boy's sea monkeys he had once. They weren't really monkeys, but a kind of tiny shrimp with a million wiggly legs. I was leery of drinking water for a week thinking he'd put them in my cup. Gram and Aunt Kitty laughed.

"Oh, Holly, the aliens we're talking about are mostly plants and animals," said Aunt Kitty. "Invasive species are not native to this land, they were brought here from other countries. They're not outer space aliens." Gram chuckled and put her arm around my shoulders. The twins howled with laughter.

"After we take the scenic drive we're heading to the beach to meet my friend Pearl Walker, the Park Ranger," giggled Aunt Kitty. "She can tell you more about these aliens."

Alligator Hill
Ovens

Pierce
Stocking Drive

PIERCE STOCKING'S DRIVE

As we turned off the main road Aunt Kitty announced, "This is Pierce Stocking Drive, kids."

"Sounds like one of your socks, Holly—you know, pierced stockings," Sie grinned. I poked her in the ribs.

"Maybe they named it that because your socks get worn out from climbing this high up," I said.

"Actually, Pierce Stocking was a man who spent his life in Michigan's forests," said Aunt Kitty. "When he was young he worked as a lumberman and learned to loved the woods. He taught himself a lot about nature."

"Awesome, just like Cousin Pauline Bunyan. She worked in a lumber camp and loved the trees too," I said.

"Pierce loved the view of the islands, dunes and Lake Michigan and wanted to share it with others, so he came up with the idea for this road," Aunt Kitty continued.

Gram drove as Aunt Kitty read to us from the brochure about what we saw. The old van was unhappy and chugged in protest up the long steep hill. We stopped at the top to let it catch its breath. Black and white woodpeckers of different sizes flitted through the trees.

We parked the van near an overlook with a tower. There we saw everything Pierce Stocking had loved; the dunes, the lake, the islands. It was a gull's eye view of the park. As far west as we could see, there was nothing but blue. Blue sky met blue water. It was awesome times ten.

Sleeping Bear
Dune Overlook

"I remembered my teacher telling us that the Great Lakes hold one third of the world's fresh water supply," T said.

"That's a lot of water, and a lot of sand," I said. Lake Michigan made me thirsty just looking at it. Sie snapped pictures of the overlook view.

"I wanted you girls to see the big picture of the big lake," said Gram. "Lake Michigan is the second biggest Great Lake, next to the Upper Peninsula's Lake Superior."

"Wow, it sure is a big picture," said T.

"There are the Manitou Islands," pointed Aunt Kitty. Shimmering in the distance they looked like bears stretched out and kicking back, floating in a giant crystal blue pool. I smiled at that thought.

"I see why Sleeping Bear Dunes got named the most beautiful place in the U.S.," remarked Gram. "Thanks to Pierce's love of the land we can all experience this amazing view."

"How did all of this sand get here?" asked T.

"The short explanation is that the glaciers dumped it here when they

10,000 years ago

MelTiNg GlaCieRs + Wind x Sand = DUNES!

1-Mile-Tall-Glacier-Cake: Clay, boulders, soil, sand

receded thousands of years ago, then the winds piled the sand up creating dunes," said Aunt Kitty.

"Where's the mom bear, Misha-Makwa?" T asked, looking around.

"She's right in front of us, just off to the right." Gram pointed at a small wooded hill perched atop the dune. From there Misha-Makwa had a clear view of her island cubs.

"No wonder Misha-Makwa's cubs couldn't make it," I said.

"I wouldn't be able to swim halfway to the islands, let alone to another shore that we can't even see."

"Too bad the bears didn't have boats to paddle across in, like those kayaks," said T sadly, pointing at the tiny boats out on the great water.

"Kayaks! I wanna ride in a kayak," I said. "They look like fun."

"They are and you will," said Aunt Kitty. "Pearl and I will be doing water testing out at Otter Lake tomorrow. We're getting some kayaks rounded up for you to use out there."

"Awesome adventure, times three!" I shrieked.

"How do you test water?" T asked Aunt Kitty.

"Put it in a soda bottle and give it a pop quiz," joked Sie. We all groaned and got back in the van.

"That's very clever Miss Sierra," giggled Aunt Kitty, "and you are mostly right. We collect it in plastic bags and and test it for harmful bacteria."

Gram turned the key but the engine hesitated. "Come on old girl," she said. Finally, and with much protest, it started. We rolled down the hill. "I'm glad it's downhill all the way, she may never get back up again."

When we got to the park beach in Empire the van sputtered and stopped.

"Well, it was the end of the road anyway," Aunt Kitty chirped. "There's Ranger Pearl over there. I'm sure she can get some help for us from the park folks." T and Sie and I walked around to where Gram was scratching her head.

"That's weird," she said. "We have a flat tire, too. Some luck."

Sie turned to me, "Good luck charm, eh?"

BEACH BUMMING

People on the beach waded and splashed in the turquoise glass waves that rolled to shore. The lake looked fine to me. It was hard to believe that there were water problems in the Park.

"So this is Lake Michigan," I said touching the water.

"You're weird, Holly. It's the same lake we swam in on Beaver Island," said Sie.

"Yeah, but it seems different here."

A tall woman in a National Park Service uniform of green pants and an olive shirt came toward us in long strides. She had large glasses that covered half of her face and a Smokey Bear-style hat. I've always wanted a hat like that.

"Pearl Walker's my name. Lake Michigan's my game," she said, snorting at her joke, and shook Gram's and Aunt Kitty's hands. She looked like a Great blue heron, tall and thin with short wisps of dark graying hair. Her huge glasses made her nose look like a beak. She gripped her belt with both hands as she walked up to us. I thought we were in trouble.

"Welcome to the Sleeping Bear Dunes National Lakeshore, ladies," she said, and with a quick smile for each of us shook our hands. "And welcome to Alien Invaders 101."

Sie nudged me. "Sounds like a video game."

"Yes, indeedy, we have a lot of work to do. A lot." Pearl raised her eyebrows. "I see that you've brought your team of volunteers with you, Kitty. The more the merrier!" she said eyeballing us.

The twins cringed. They had expected fun and relaxing vacation, not work.

"My job here at this fine park is to protect our shores and water. I like to think of it as H.O.M.E.S. Land Security, as in lakes Huron, Ontario, Michigan, Erie, and Superior— H.O.M.E.S. Keeping our H.O.M.E.S. clean and pristine," she said, hoisting up her belt.

"I trust that your aunt has given you the lowdown on the park being invaded by aliens. As volunteers, it's our duty to take them out. One by one." She nodded toward a pile of full plastic garbage bags nearby. A few people were picking plants with purple fringy flowers. T gulped at the pile of bags.

"Invasive species. My job is your job," said Pearl. "What I say is, 'Make my day' to any alien who comes my way! Today we are hunting for the dreaded baby's breath."

"Baby's breath is dangerous? Wait till I tell my little sister that one," joked Sie.

"How do the plants get here?" asked T.

"The seeds come in on the water, in the air and on your boots," said Pearl. "They get around. When they find an empty place they fill it. They can be annoying and extremely difficult to get rid of."

"Sounds like Ivy Buckthorn's family," snickered Sie.

"Not only can aliens be plants but animals and insects too," said Aunt Kitty.

"Ladies, get to know thy enemy." Pearl whipped out a wanted poster with strange creatures and plants.

"Holy creeps! I didn't know there were so many," I whistled, looking at the chart. We had our work cut out for us—for like ten years.

"Invasive species come from other places and out-compete native plants and animals because the invasive species don't have any natural enemies in their new home," Pearl explained. "Because they have no natural enemies or predators in their new

home, nothing eats them and their population gets out of control. This becomes a problem for native species.

"For instance, here are some striped aquatic aliens who live in the water." Pearl picked up a long strand of tangled weeds covered with striped triangular shells and handed it to T.

"Zebra mussels. They're a menace to lake and land."

"These tiny things cause damage?" asked T. "Each one's only as big as my thumbnail."

"The answer is in your hands Miss Tierra," said Aunt Kitty. "There are far too many mussels in the lake and they attach themselves to plants, boats, docks, calling anything solid home. One female can lay up to a million eggs a year."

"That's a lot of babies," said Sie. "When millions of mussels lay millions of eggs, that's a gazillion aliens."

"The mussels filter tiny plant food particles from the water, called phytoplankton," said Pearl. "When there are too many mussels, they remove too much phytoplankton. One of the problems this creates is that the native fish, whose babies rely on that food source, have a harder time surviving."

"When life becomes out of balance, bad things happen," said Gram. "Zebra mussels affect everything that relies on the lake for survival—loons, plovers, gulls, ducks, fish. The food chain links everyone."

"Who would think such a big lake could have such big problems," I said. "Aliens are big trouble."

"And guess who's at the top of the food chain, guys? We are. So we all need to work to solve this problem," said Pearl.

"How can we solve the problem? We're just kids," said T.

"Learn more about the lake, and how to keep it clean," said Pearl, handing each of us a bag, rubber gloves and a clipboard.

"We're already trained to do invasive plant removal, so you girls get to fill these bags with beach garbage—another beach invasive," Aunt Kitty winked at us. "We'll meet back here in an hour. Then we can enjoy the lake!"

"Remember, ladies, nab it—zap it—nip it in the bud!" Pearl called to us. "To pick, pull and pluck is to serve and protect."

Be A Super Lake, SUPER HERO!
Help wipe out ALIEN INVADERS!

zebra mussel

round goby

Alien ANIMALS

spiny waterflea

Alien PLANTS

spotted knapweed

baby's breath

eurasian milfoil

BERNIE THE BEACH GUARDIAN

"Looks like a popular picnicking place," said Sie, as we headed down the beach with our bags. T studied the clipboard. We had a chart of expected beach litter finds and room for other unusual trash. We were to keep track of what we gathered by marking the trash on the chart. As acting GeEK secretary she always took neat notes and, with her glitter pens, colorful ones at that, so T was in charge of the clipboard.

We decided to fill one bag at a time, and saved one to use for driftwood, shells and other treasures.

Sie picked up a bottle cap and dropped it in our bag. T checked off the find on the sheet.

"It's kinda like trick-or-treating," said T. When we thought of it that way, we got excited and looked harder. We had been collecting trash for a while when I realized someone was following us.

It was boy our age, kinda chunky and dark haired. He wore baggy basketball shorts and a black oversized t-shirt with fish on it. A beach towel was tied around his neck like a super hero cape. He had a pair of swim goggles on his head and carried his own bag of trash. He sort of looked like an alien.

"Let's take a break and see what we have," suggested Sie. We moved over to a log near some towering dune grasses. The Team

looked over T's litter collecting notes while I wiggled my toes
in the sand. I watched the grains move in the wind. I pulled out
my magnifier card to look at the sand up close. I never knew

RAiNBOWS of SaND!
- quartz (clear)
- garnet (red)
- magnetite (black)
- epidote (green)
- feldspar (tans)

that sand could be so many colors. I thought it was just tan. I jotted down observations and poured a sample into my field note journal.

Sie read from the list: "35 cigarette filters. Gross. 29 bottle caps, 5 pop cans, 14 food wrappers and 2 styrofoam cartons, 4 spoons, a broken fork, 4 straws, 5 gum wrappers, 6 water bottles and a bouquet of 6 popped, pink party balloons on purple streamers knotted with grasses."

"A bird could get tangled in that," said T, shaking her head. "If people wouldn't throw stuff down then we wouldn't have to pick it up."

"Yeah, why do *we* have to clean up the shore? We don't live here. We're just visiting," said Sie.

"It's a shame for us who do live here to have to see it," said the alien boy in his cape, moving over to us. "I didn't mean to listen in, but thanks for helping us. Lots of people use the lakes and have fun. Not many help keep them clean or protect them."

Sie looked down at her feet. "Uh, sorry for what I said."

"No biggie," he said with a grin. "I say if folks use the lake they should be guardians and protect it, so I dub thee Guardians! That's what I am. Bernie Walker's the name, the lakes are my game." His eyes twinkled as he shot out his hand for us to shake.

"Hey, are you...?" Sie began.

"Yep, Ranger Pearl's nephew. I see you met my Auntie," he said, pointing at our garbage bags. "She gives those to everyone she meets. My aunt and I live here in town," he smiled. "Every morning I come down to the beach and comb for buried treasure. I like to think of myself as a super hero/lake guardian—like Aqua Man," he said proudly.

"I'm Holly, this is Sierra and Tierra. We three are GeEKS, Geo Explorer Kids. It's our first time to Sleeping Bear Dunes. My aunt knows your aunt."

"GeEKs and Guardians," he laughed and bowed. "We'll make an awesome, cool team. So didja find anything good—other than trash?"

"Sierra found cool driftwood that looks like a woodpecker. Tierra found a wooden marble and I found this faded black feather with two white spots," I showed Bernie our finds.

"Dig it! A loon feather!" he said. "Anything else?" Sie shrugged and showed him the litter list.

"Bottle caps, water bottles, plastic fast food ice cream sundae cups with lids! Excellent! I can use all of those." It was like Christmas Day for Bernie. The only other person I ever saw that excited about stuff like that was...well, me!

"What do you need them for?" asked Sie.

"The things I find are like artifacts. I make stuff with them.

Sometimes art, sometimes useful things. I've been collecting ever since I could walk."

Holy creeps! This kid and I spoke the same language.

Gram and Ranger Pearl came up the beach and we waved at them. "Kitty is getting the van looked at by some Park people," said Gram. I had forgotten about the van troubles.

"Say, are you guys thirsty? Want to see my house? It's right over there," said Bernie.

Now he was speaking T's language. Her eyes got big. "I could go for a drink."

"Tourists tromp and locals love. Many visitors litter and leave," he said as we walked to his house. "I don't think they'd like it if we went to their homes and tossed garbage and pollution in their water."

As we walked along I patted my good luck claw-tifact. It was good luck to find Bernie.

BeAchCombiNg
for the GoOd,
the Bad &
the Ugly

BERNIE'S DIGS

The small, tidy white house stood in town among wildflowers and swaying dune grasses. There were bird feeders hanging among the trees in the yard.

Inside, a library of books lined the walls. Pearl's desk was tucked in next to the couch. Sierra went crazy over Pearl's weather station equipment as we passed through the kitchen. On a plate on the table was a sandwich pierced with a straw and a note attached. It looked like a PBJ sailboat! "Have a happy day, love Auntie" the sail note read.

When we got to his room we saw his name was spelled out in shells on a sign on his door. The sign clattered as he swung the door wide. His room was any Geo-Explorer Kid's dream. Heck, it was a biologist's and Harry Potter's dream all rolled into one. I stood with my mouth hanging open like the largemouth bass in the poster on his wall.

"Holy creeps!" was all I could manage to get out. It was coolness times ten.

"This is my research headquarters," he said proudly.

Posters, boxes and books lined the walls. Shelves of jars held different things—bones, stones, bottle caps, beach glass. The door to his closet was open. That's where his bed was, a cot piled high with clothes and stacks of comic books. A long table held fossils, microscopes and bubbling tanks of fish. "And these are my specimens. They're really pets, too," Bernie said. "The orange fish is Zoomer, he's a comet. He jumps a lot so I have to keep him covered. The brown goggle-eyed one is Pig, he eats a lot."

"Aww!" squealed T with glee. She was peeking into the tall aquarium of plants.

"That's Lightning, my pet gecko. He's arboreal, meaning he climbs trees and likes to hide."

Sie was checking out the gadgets and tools on his desk as I inspected a jar labeled "Sea Monsters—DO NOT DRINK". There was an open notebook of scribbled drawings nearby.

"They're no bigger than a grain of rice," said Sie squinting at them. "How can they be sea monsters?"

"They aren't really sea monsters. They're called triops," he explained. "Those guys have been around for 70 million years. I like old, ancient things."

"So do I!" I blurted.

"Triops eggs stay around a long time. If their pond dries up, the eggs wait until it rains again to hatch. That's what I'm afraid is going to happen out at Bass Lake."

"What's wrong with Bass Lake?" I asked. "Is this the water problem my Aunt Kitty is here to help with?"

"Yes it is," he said. "The water level has been dropping in

that lake since early spring. You guys want to help me find out why?"

"Sure we would!" I answered for the Team. I looked over at the twins, who were staring at me and snickering softly. I felt my freckles burn. Bernie pulled out a map of the park and pointed to a few small lakes. Otter was the largest, then Bass and Deer, the smallest.

"Auntie Pearl and I have been doing water testing there and noticed the lake level dropping. If Bass Lake dries up, it will affect Otter Lake."

"What about Lake Michigan?" asked Sie, pointing to the creek that leads from Otter Lake to the big lake. "Does Bass Lake get its water from Lake Michigan?"

"No," he said, "it's the other way around. Deer, Bass and Otter Lakes feed Lake Michigan. Levels in all the lakes go up and down all the time, but this summer they have dropped a lot at Bass Lake."

"Maybe we can go out there and see," I said. "Aunt Kitty did say that we were going to do water testing at Otter Lake tomorrow morning."

"Sweet," said Bernie. "We'll get to the bottom of this."

"Bottom, lake bottom, get it?" I said, laughing too loud. The Team stared at me. "Never mind."

I studied a picture on the wall of a family with a fish. "Talk about ancient. That's a really old photo and one big fish."

"That's my grandpa when he was a boy. He caught that sturgeon. The Odawa Indian name for it is Nahma, Spirit of the Lake. I'm Odawa, bear clan."

"I've never heard of a sturgeon," said T.

"It's an ancient fish, kinda like a living fossil," Bernie said.

"It's lived here for millions of years. The old guys used spears to catch them. I just like to study them. I'm raising a sturgeon right now, to be released into the wild this Friday. His name is Stumpy 'cuz he doesn't have a tail."

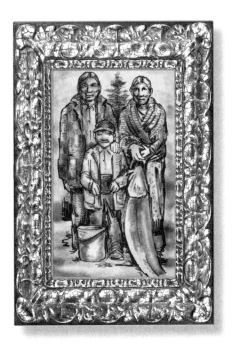

"Where is it, this "Nah-may" sturgeon?" I asked. "Can we see it?"

"He's in a tank in a trailer not far from here in Manistee, with some other young Nahma. I get to release him into the Manistee River. Wanna come watch?"

"Sure!" I yelped. We heard a honk outside. Gram had the van running again.

"Dig it! So tomorrow we study the lakes," he said as he walked us to the door. "And don't forget, Friday is Stumpy's big day. Then Saturday is The Sleeping Bear Dunes Park Adoption Week Picnic," he hollered as Sie and T hopped into the van.

"He sure is a super cool, super hero lake guardian kid," I said, smiling, and turned around too quickly, slamming into the van door.

NIGHT-BEAR NIGHTMARES?

"Time to get moving girls," Gram said, tapping on our door. I yawned and sat up. The twins must've let me sleep in, since their beds were empty. "Hurry, Holly, we're meeting Ranger Pearl this afternoon."

I grabbed my bag and ran into the yard. But I froze when I found myself surrounded by bears. My heart stopped. I couldn't breathe. Bears of all sizes milled about the farm buildings.

"Just in time for the picnic, Holly," Aunt Kitty stretched out her hand. "How good of you to join us." I looked around and recognized Wild relatives from old photos. Great Aunt Daisy Crockett was playing horseshoes with a family of black bears. Pauline Bunyan, my Wild "Yooper" cousin, was flipping pancakes on a griddle. Bears were licking their chops and holding dinner plates in their paws. It was like the "Teddy Bear Picnic" that Mom sang to me as a child. I could hear the words and the music.

If you go out in the woods today
You're sure of a big surprise.
If you go out in the woods today
You'd better go in disguise.
For every bear that ever there was
Will gather there for certain, because
Today's the day the teddy bears have their picnic.

Aunt Jenny Appleseed offered Gram a slice of her Apple Brown Betty. Aunt Kitty casually chatted with bears at the picnic table, exchanging recipes. Aunt Jenny gave a hug and huge slice of her dessert to a large, sad looking black bear. The bear looked like the illustration of Misha-Makwa, the mother bear, from my book. It gobbled the treat down quicker than Hunter, then ambled off into the fog.

"Here, Holly, we saved a seat for you," called Gram.

"No thanks. I'm good right here," I said. What was going on? Two cinnamon-colored bear cubs chased each other, playing tag. They came barreling up to me. "Tag! You're it!" the smallest cub hit me hard on my head.

That's when a large, grinning, eight-legged bear floated toward me like a glowing balloon.

"Holy creeps!" I yelled and bolted upright.

"Holly! Another nightmare?"

asked T.

"No," I said, gasping as I woke up. "Well, sort of."

"Was T's underwear attacking you again?" Sie snickered, gathering her toothbrush and clothes from the dresser.

"It was terrifying. There was a picnic, pie, and singing."

"That sounds horrible," Sie joked.

"No, there were singing bears," I said. "It was the Teddy Bear Picnic." The girls rolled backwards on their beds laughing. I stood there feeling like a dweeb.

"Teddy bears?" chortled Sie.

"I hoped my night-bear nightmares were done," I said, getting my claw-tifact out from my pillow. "I mean, I thought I had my run-in with a bear the first night here. Now I'm not so sure," I said, looking at the stone.

"I need to consult an expert on bears," I said, sticking it into my pocket. "I'll ask Bernie, he seems to know a lot about local wildlife and legends—and he's bear clan." The twins chuckled. "What?" I asked. But they just giggled.

After breakfast we ran into Bernie and Pearl at the grocery store buying snacks for our trip to Otter Lake.

"I'm heading over to the park HQ to pick up kayaks if you girls want to stop by and look around," said Pearl flashing us a quick grin.

"Sure would," I said and patted the stone in my pocket. "I need to know more about the dunes and the Sleeping Bear." Just then we heard a crunching crash and a loud wailing whine.

"Someone has their hands full," smirked Gram, as a clerk rushed to the back of the store. The wail caused the hair on my neck to rise. My freckles sizzled and my skin itched. Only one thing on this green earth could make such a vile commotion.

Around the corner came a raging Ivy Buckthorn.

"What?" Sie gasped. I was stunned. Ivy shoved past me and towards the door. Then she turned and looked back at us. She snorted in disgust, narrowed her eyes to slits, then stormed off in a huff. Mrs. Buckthorn was talking with the clerk and paying for their things.

"At least we're not on an island this time," said T. "We can only hope that she and her family are passing through on their way home."

What was it with the Buckthorn family anyway? They were such an invasive species themselves. They were annoying, everywhere and impossible to get rid of. Even on vacation. Living next to them in Hayfields was one thing, but running into them twice on vacation was another. I'd rather run in to ghosts or aliens.

"How's that good luck charm of yours working now, Holly?" Sie joked.

GONE FISHING

We followed the Walkers to the Philip A. Hart Visitor Center. While we waited for the boats to get loaded up we looked at the giant relief map of the entire park. Gram pointed out the islands and Misha-Makwa. Seeing her this size she didn't seem so scary. We went through the gift shop before going in to the interpretive exhibits. I wanted to learn about and feel the rocks on display there.

"My grandpa used to tell me that rocks talk," said Bernie. "They tell you things. So I listen every time I pick one up." This was my cue. I pulled out my pink stone claw-tifact.

"I found this the day we got here!" I blurted. I held out the palm-sized pinkish knife-like curved stone. "I think it looks like a fossilized bear claw." Bernie silently examined it.

"Dig it, it does look like a big claw," he finally said, grinning.

"Ever since I got to the park I've had weird dreams." I felt all wiggly and embarrassed.

"What kind of dreams?" he asked. Of course, this is when T and Sie walked over to us.

"About singing underwear and teddy bears," joked Sierra. I shot her a look.

"A bear did sing to me. It placed a paw on my forehead and sang 'The Teddy Bear Picnic' song," I said, my freckles sizzling in embarassment.

"I believe you," said Bernie, "Gramps always said listen to your dreams."

"Does this mean a bear is really stalking me? A ghost bear? Or Misha-Makwa?"

Bernie shrugged. "I don't know. Could be. Bear are powerful symbols. I guess I'd listen to her when she speaks, though. Bears have always been the police watching over territory, the guardians of the people."

"Are there really ghosts in the dunes?" asked Sie.

"Sure, a whole ghost forest is buried in the dunes," Bernie said. "Dead trees sticking out all over. The sand covered them up and killed them, then they were uncovered again. It's like the dunes are walking or moving."

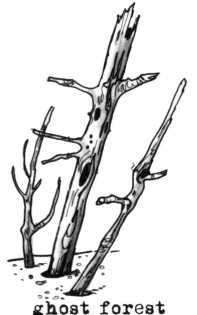

ghost forest

"What about Misha-Makwa? Does she haunt the dunes?" asked T.

"I don't know, but the legend says that she waits for her cubs. Gramps used to say stories aren't just stories."

"Kids, we're heading to the lake!" Gram called. "We've got the boats loaded up and we're ready to roll."

"Dig it," I said. "Adventure, times four!"

When we got to Otter Lake, Aunt Kitty, Gram and Ranger Pearl unloaded the kayaks and canoe. The twins slathered on greasy sunscreen. We grabbed life jackets and paddles and carried everything to the water's edge. Dragonflies and damselflies zipped about nabbing bugs on the wing.

"Look at the shells in the water," said T. "Zebra stripes!"

"Yikes! There're here too!"

"That's how invasive species are. They get everywhere people are. If boats are in a lake where there are zebra mussels the eggs can stick to the boat and be transferred to another lake," explained Aunt Kitty.

T and Sie got into a park canoe. I got Aunt Kitty's red kayak. It had more stickers on it than her car. Bernie had his own kayak. Ranger Pearl and Aunt Kitty shoved us out into the shallow water. Then they grabbed their water testing gear and gadgets and paddled out in the other park canoe.

"I love my 'yak. I can skim over the water like a water strider," said Bernie.

"A what?" asked T, dipping her paddle into the lake.

"A long-legged bug that walks on the water," I said, grinning at Bernie. Sie shook her head.

 I got comfy in Aunt Kitty's red kayak. It was different than the canoe I'd been in before. It felt more stable.

"Meet back here in an hour, kids," Gram called. She stretched out on a beach chair in the sun on the sandy birch and cedar shore, moving the cooler over to prop her feet up.

The lake was quiet until we heard a high-pitched peeping sound overhead.

"Eagle!" said Bernie, pointing up. "There!" It looked like a large hawk coming near.

"It doesn't have a white head or tail," said Sie, getting her camera ready.

"It's a young one. They have dark heads and splotchy tail feathers," Bernie explained. The eagle was huge for being a young bird. It swept gracefully over the trees and out over the water. That's when we noticed that it had a fish in its talons and was being chased by another large bird. This one was mostly white from below.

Great Blue
Heron

Osprey

Kingfisher

Common Loon

Bald
Eagle

FISHING BIRDS!

What "tool" does each use?
Beak or Talon? Color each bird for
your own wetland bird field guide!

"Osprey," said Bernie. "It's going to try to take that eagle's lunch." We watched the aerial display of circling and diving birds until they took their scuffle over to a neighboring lake.

"That's mean," said T, shading her eyes.

"That's life," said Bernie. "It's all about survival."

"I wonder who will win," I said.

T took a swig from her water bottle. "It's pretty hot. I hope I don't run out of water," she said.

"Me too," laughed Bernie. "We all need water. That's why we're worried about the level dropping. This is the largest of these three lakes that connect to Lake Michigan by Otter Creek. The level here has dropped a bit but Bass Lake has gone down even more. We can't figure out what's happening."

"Is there a leak in the lake?" asked T. "You know like a bathtub stopper was pulled?"

"I don't know," Bernie said, getting out his own scientific equipment. A pop bottle full of sand tied to a rope. "This measures the depth."

He dropped the weighted bottle into the water and held the string and let it sink. We watched it until we couldn't see it any longer. When it hit bottom he marked the string with tape. He pulled it up and measured it. "Another half inch. I wonder how much more Bass Lake has dropped. If this keeps up the lake could be in real trouble."

"Lots of animals depend on it. Look," T pointed at the sky. The eagle had come back. It had its fish and perched up high in a tall pine for lunch.

"Hey, I'm gonna go fishing, too!" I said, "I've been waiting to try out my portable pop bottle fishing kit!" I had forgotten that I had brought it along in my new, old backpack when we went

to Beaver Island.
I dug down to the
bottom and pulled
it out. It has fishing
line wrapped around
a plastic bottle.
Inside are my extra
poppers and lures.
Rubber banded to
the outside is one
of Gram's old pill
bottles where I store
a cork bobber and tiny hooks. I tied a tiny green rubber spider
lure and swivel to the line and used the rubber band to attach
the bobber. I tossed the line into the water and every so often
wiggled the spider.

The sky was so blue it hurt my eyes. A kingfisher the color
of the sky cackled and dove. It came out of the water holding a
tiny fish and sat on a branch while it ate. We floated in the sun
and ate snacks, enjoying the day. Cedars, white birches and lacy
ferns lined the shore. Suddenly the water splashed.

"H-hey, I have a fish!" I yelled. I was so surprised and excited
that I actually had caught a fish that I yanked hard on the line.
Too hard. The small green and white bass came zipping out
of the water and right at my face. All I saw was its wide-open
bucket mouth coming at me. I yelled and ducked as it fell off
the hook and into my kayak. It dropped behind me onto my
seat and was flipping around. I could hear the fish flopping as
I frantically crawled around in the rocking kayak to keep from
squishing it.

I tried sweeping the gasping fish out with one hand while trying to not tip the kayak with the other. I was tangled in fishing line with the spider lure firmly hooked to my hat. Finally, the

fish flipped out on its own with a splash. The kingfisher sat nearby in its tree. I'm sure it was laughing at me, since everyone else was. My heart was pounding and I was trapped in a web of fishing line.

"I should call *you* Water Strider," said Bernie smiling. T was holding her gut trying to catch her breath.

"Your kit works really well," chuckled Sie. "It seems you've caught yourself!"

I tried to get the spider lure out of my hat but it was stuck good. Since I don't have a knife, I had to use my claw-tifact to cut the line. That ended my fishing for the day. My face felt sunburned. The kingfisher chortled his song and flew off.

"Good thing I had my good luck stone so I could free myself," I said as I packed away my gear.

Otter Lake

GOOD LUCK CHARM?

"I don't know. It sure seems like you're not having good luck," said T, taking the final swig from her bottle. We were paddling around and gathering old skins that dragonflies had shed that were still clinging to the reeds. T wanted them for earrings. We weren't very far from where the eagle and osprey had flown when I heard a low, muffled growling sound.

"Listen. What's that noise?" I looked around. "Is that a bear?"

"Everything's a bear to you, Holly," Sie teased. Then the noise stopped.

"I don't hear anything," T said. "My water's gone. Do you think the water looks clear enough to fill my bottle?"

ghost dragonfly nymph skin

"NO!" Bernie yelled. T froze. "You can't do that. There are tiny bugs and bacteria in the water—so small that you can't see them—that can make you really sick. So while the water might look clean enough to drink, you can't without filtering or purifying it first."

"But I'm real thirsty," whined T.

Bernie pulled out a pack of Smarties and popped a pink one into his mouth. "Want one?"

"Um, OK. I guess it'll help," T said, reaching for the yellow candy he held out.

"Just one of the many treasures I found on the beach," said Bernie. T's eyes got big, but she shrugged and ate it.

"Have you found anything really, really cool? Like money or old ship parts?" Sie asked.

"Yeah, bits and bones and junk that washes up—probably from Wisconsin," he said.

Our kayaks drifted near the shore when I heard the low noise growling again. This time the Team heard it too. There was a dog barking somewhere in the woods. Then it stopped.

"Are you sure it's not a bear growling?" I asked Bernie.

"No, I don't think so," he said. "And actually, it sounds like it's coming from the other lake. Hmm. There are a few old cabins over there. Guardians, we should go investigate." He smiled. I liked how this kid thought.

We paddled our kayaks and canoe back to shore. Gram yelled to us. "Hey, campers, have fun? I was starting to think your weren't coming back." Gram hauled us ashore while Aunt Kitty and Ranger Pearl were eating lunch on the over-turned park canoe.

"Say, Auntie Pearl," said Bernie. "Can we take the Team over to Bass Lake and show it to them?"

"Sure, I haven't done water testing there yet. That sounds like a mighty fine plan," she said. After our lunch of sandwiches and fruit salad, Ranger Pearl and Aunt Kitty loaded up the boats for the trip over to Bass Lake.

This time we kids piled into one of the canoes while Aunt Kitty and Ranger Pearl took the other.

"We'll meet back here in an hour," said Gram. "No more

dancing around in the boat, Holly." Bernie snickered and the twins guffawed. My freckles sizzled.

"Of course, I don't hear that noise now," I said as we paddled near the fern-covered shore. "But my good luck claw-tifact will help us." There were a few old run down cabins set back among the trees.

"Those cabins look abandoned." Our heads turned as the young eagle came back. It soared over the pines and gave a peeping cry. Right then we heard a dog bark.

"Follow that eagle," said Bernie. "Where there are eagles, there are small animals." Sure enough, among thick ferns there stood a weathered dock. A small dog yipped and yapped.

"I know this place," said Bernie. "The Parkers used to summer here." We paddled along the sandy edge among the lily pads. Tucked among the dark pines and cedars was a small white cottage.

I should have put on some sunscreen, my arms were itching. In fact, I began to itch all over. Squinting into the bright light, I spotted someone in the yard in a blue and yellow floral sundress watering the lawn with a hose.

"Do you know her?" I asked, scratching under my hat.

"Naw, lots of folks are turning their cabins into rental cottages," whispered Bernie. The girl went into the cottage, slamming the door, and the dog started barking. The yapping little beast came running out from behind a shed toward the dock. My skin crawled. I'd recognize that mangy white poodle just about anywhere.

"Holy creeps!" I clapped my hand over my mouth. The girl was Ivy Buckthorn and the yapping dog was her annoying poodle, Queenie.

"Queenie! Get back here now!" Ivy screeched as she burst back out the door. "You know you're not supposed to walk on the grass. Daddy just poisoned the weeds on it. You'll get sick."

Just Say NO! to Poisons!

We tried to back up the canoe but it got jammed in the lily pads. It was too late to get away. Ivy Buckthorn was already standing on the dock.

"If it's not Stinkberry Shortstuff and the Power Puff girls." Ivy is creative when it comes to making fun of people—especially people with red hair and freckles that are me.

"I see you know each other," Bernie laughed.

I knew Ivy Buckthorn was mean and nasty and mean. And I knew I try to stay as far from her as possible. But other than that I didn't really know her at all.

"Sorry kid, I don't know you well enough to make fun of you yet," Ivy sneered at Bernie, who smiled back at her.

"I thought her family would've been long gone after the Beaver Island incident," whispered Sie. Ivy scowled and crossed her arms. Queenie yapped louder, nearly falling over the dock edge. Ivy scooped up the shaking dog.

"If you come up here, I'll sick my dog on you," she yelled.

"That thing? said Bernie.

"She's fierce," snapped Ivy. I was worried more about Ivy biting us than Queenie.

"So, did you guys move here?" I asked her, trying not to sound too hopeful.

"Don't be a dummy, we're on vacation. Mother needs rest and Daddy is working here. The bigger question is, what the heck are you freaks doing here? Are you spying on us?"

"No, we were out for canoe ride and heard all the barking," said Bernie.

"It was you who got my dog barking and that might wake my mother so shove off, sailor." Ivy carried Queenie back to the house and dropped her inside. While we tried to get the canoe unstuck she came back to the dock with a bowl. A goldfish swam in circles gasping at the top of the murky water.

"You still here, Smellberry?" Ivy scowled.

"What are you doing with that?" asked Bernie. Ivy looked at the bowl.

"I'm setting Fluffy free, let him run with the wild fish. He's too much to take care of. Besides, he's pretty stupid and boring.

All he does is float around all day," she said, peeling her lips back, revealing many sharp teeth in an evil smile.

"No!" said Bernie. "You can't just dump him in here—he doesn't belong here."

"Whatever, twerp, my daddy gave him to me as a pet, when what I wanted was a little kitty. So if you won't let me dump him in the lake then *you* take him," she growled.

"OK," said Bernie. She set the bowl on the dock and moved it to the edge with her toe. We pulled up closer to the dock and T reached over to grab the desperate looking fish.

"Nice knowin' ya, Fluffmeister. Have a good life," Ivy said. Then she whipped around, her ponytail cutting the air like a machete, and marched back into the cottage. T held the bowl in her lap as we turned the canoe around and paddled back.

"That was weird. She didn't even try to hurt us," I said.

"Ivy's never been nice before," said Sie, "to anything."

TROUBLE TIMES TWO!

"Wash day kids," said Gram. "The house has no washing machine, so we're using a bucket and teamwork." We each washed our clothes in cold water in one bucket and rinsed them in another. Gram went back inside to do her washing in the sink. I think she knew we would all end up wet.

"I was disappointed that we didn't find the source of the noise but that we *did* find Ivy and Queenie," I said wringing out my socks. No holes yet.

"Yeah, when Ivy's family is around that spells trouble," said T, pinning her t-shirt to the line.

"I'm thinking you need to trade in your good luck charm for something else. Like something that actually gives you good luck," said Sie.

Gram came out of the house with an armload of dripping clothes. "We're washing today because tomorrow we get to visit the little cub, South Manitou Island," Gram said, hanging up her concert t-shirt.

"Awesome!" I cried. "We get to visit the little cub. How's that for good luck, Sie?" I patted my pocket with the claw-tifact to make sure it was safe.

Sie shrugged. "We'll see Holly." I tossed a wet sock at her, which started a wet laundry fight.

After dinner we brought in our dry laundry and then sat outside listening to the owl songs. Aunt Kitty came out with freshly popped popcorn.

"Lime-with-cayenne pepper-and-garlic-onion-flavored popcorn anyone?" T cringed.

"Did you find anything out about the lake levels today, Aunt Kitty?" I asked, popping tasty, tangy kernels into my mouth.

"Not really. We checked for water clarity and depth," she said. Hunter was busy sniffing around the corner of the house. When he realized that there was food he nearly sat on Aunt Kitty's lap. "Otter Lake levels have dropped some more, but Bass Lake dropped a lot. It's losing more water each day, Pearl says. It's very disturbing."

"Yeah, having Buckthorns on the lake would make anything dry up," joked Sie, wiping seasoning off her corn.

After we finished off our snack we all headed to bed. I put my good luck stone in my pillowcase.

"I hope you have good dreams tonight," said T.

"I think it was just a fluke, the nightmare last night," I said. "Besides, Bernie said to listen to my dreams. So I'm ready for whatever Momma Bear has to say." I made sure I had my flashlight and waited for sleep to come. The girls dropped off right away. I could feel my sunburn burning but I drifted off to sleep eventually.

"No-o!" I yelled, "Stop!" I sat up and held my head.

"A simple 'Good morning' would do," said Sie, rubbing her eyes. "Was a bear attacking you again?"

"Not really," I said scratching my arms. "Misha-Makwa's

attacking me with singing and dancing gummy bear nightmares. They keep singing it over and over."

"'The Teddy Bear Picnic' song?" T asked, sitting up.

"Are you sure that you didn't drink some kind of invasive brain worm larva or something?" Sie slid on her glasses and looked at me. "Whoa, Holly," she said. "You look weird! Like an alien or a cherry gummy bear." My face did feel funny. T handed me her mirror.

"Holy creeps! My head is all swelled up!" I said. I pushed on my forehead. It felt like a water balloon. My cheeks and lips were red and swollen and my arms too.

"Creepy," said T, poking my squishy forehead. "Must be from your sunburn."

"Or your good luck charm," said Sie. "When I got a bad sunburn in Florida, my dad made me drinks lots of water. Come on." The twins led me out into the kitchen. Gram whistled when she saw me.

"You look like a tomato," she said. She gave me allergy medicine with lots of water and sat me at the table. "You stay here and rest while we get ready." I sat with my notebook and watched everyone bustle about the kitchen.

While I watched I got sleepy. I kept hearing the dancing bears. I tried to stay awake but they kept pulling me with them. "Come on," the smallest cub said, "Mama Bear needs you." I had just dozed off when Sie shook my shoulder.

"You OK, Holly?" Sie asked. "I think the missing water from the lake is in your face." I was groggy and sat up.

"The cub was talking to me. I think the baby bear wants me to help its mother, Misha-Makwa. Maybe there will be clues on South Manitou Island."

SOUTH MANITOU ISLAND

We arrived at the dock where the park service boat of adventure sat. I was still feeling woozy from the medicine. Gram made sure that I covered myself in sunscreen.

The park service boat to South Manitou was much smaller than the *Emerald Isle* we had taken to Beaver Island. Gram

had stored my sleeping bag and pillow in a garbage bag, and I had my backpack. The twins' gear, usually tripling that of what I carried, was trimmed down to two bags each and one with blankets and pillows. Gulls circled and clouds scuttled by. The little boat rocked as the blue water rolled.

Tanned hikers in t-shirts, cargo shorts and sporty sunglasses lined up wearing backpacks covered in dangling, hi-tech camping equipment. We passed our gear to the crew to be loaded into the cargo area. The boat was taking some of us to South Manitou first, then dropping off the rest of the hikers on North Manitou, the larger bear cub island.

"This is exciting. I wonder what it'll be like over there," I said to T. I slid across the seat to be next to the window. Scientific observation.

"Even though the lake is not very rough today," said T, looking over at the churning blue water, "I still can't imagine the mother bear and her kids swimming in this."

"It's like we're a tiny bottle cap floating in the middle of a huge lake," I said, leaning my head against the window.

"We kind of are Holly," said Sie. "Lake Michigan is pretty huge." I made a tiny pillow with my hoodie. The rocking became like a cradle and the engine a lullaby. The next thing I knew T was shaking my shoulder.

"Holly, we're here," she said. I was feeling pretty shaky and fuzzy when I stood up.

"I always expected that a bear would chase me, with me being a Wild and all," I said swaying. "But the funny thing is, I'm the one chasing a bear."

"How do you hunt a legendary ghost bear?" T asked.

"Maybe you should leave that ghost bear a plate of ghost cookies," laughed Sie as we stepped off the boat.

Ranger Pearl and Bernie were already there waiting in two

golf carts on the dock. "Good morning, troopers," Pearl saluted us and flashed her smile. She came over to help us get our gear. "I'll show you your place."

I stepped off the boat and the crew handed me my bags. When I saw Bernie I smiled and waved, then teetered and nearly fell off the dock.

"Holly!" cried Gram, "Be careful!" That's when I heard a splash and the twins giggling.

"Holly, you knocked your sleeping bag into the water," T said, while Sie guffawed. There below me, under the dock, floated the garbage bag that held my pillow and sleeping bag. Thank goodness it was tied shut. I was glad I hadn't knocked my new, old backpack with all of my stuff into the water.

A sailor grabbed a long hook and snagged my bag before it headed out to the Manitou Passage. I was completely embarrassed when I handed Bernie my wet bag to load onto the golf cart.

"Hey, litterbug!" Bernie said, as he held his gut laughing.

I felt for my claw-tifact in my pocket and a moment of panic swept over me. Holy creeps, the stone was still in my pillowcase! With all of the morning's events I forgot to put it in my pocket. Now I was really glad Gram packed all my stuff into a garbage bag.

We took a short golf cart ride down the sandy road to a tiny, white house tucked into cedars on the beach.

"This is it kids. The Kramer House," said Ranger Pearl. Gram and Aunt Kitty pulled up in their golf cart next to us. My mouth hung open.

"You'll catch flies if you keep it open any longer," said Sie, "What gives Holly?"

"I had a dream on the boat about a place that looked just like this," I said. "Sandy, with ferns and cedars. A little white cottage. And a cub who kept telling me to find his mother."

We unpacked bread, oatmeal, chips and canned food into the tiny kitchen. I unloaded my gear onto the porch and opened the garbage bag to hang my sleeping bag and pillow out to dry. I reached in and grabbed my stone claw. It was still there. I sighed with relief.

"Make sure you put everything out of the reach of 'micro-bears'," said Gram, carrying bags inside.

"Yes ma'am, this place is loaded with them. 'Micro-bears' are *everywhere*," said Ranger Pearl, following Gram and Aunt Kitty with more bags.

"Wait. What's a micro-bear?" I asked. To my explorer mind it sounded like a clue.

"'Micro-bears' are chipmunks," said Bernie. "The little rascals will steal you blind."

"Even though they are cute they can become a real nuisance," said Aunt Kitty. "Once people start feeding them they hang around begging. We don't want them to come to rely on 'people food' so we keep them wild by not feeding them."

"Aunt Kitty and I are going with Pearl to work on one of the historical houses that the park is renovating," said Gram, jamming a cheese stick in her mouth while climbing into the golf cart. "It's not that far from here. You kids can take the other cart and explore if you like." They zipped off, and we had the place to ourselves!

The front yard was our first stop. Chipmunks scattered as we walked towards water.

"Let's hit the beach. Treasures are always found there," I said. T and Sie and I were flipping over stones looking for cool ones to decorate our fire pit up by the house. There were clean white bones and of course thousands of zebra mussel shells. I sketched them all in my field notebook. I looked up and found a micro-bear playing hide and seek with us near some rocks.

"Wow," cried Bernie. "Look at this huge white feather! I'll bet it came from a Trumpeter swan!"

"A trumpeting swan?" asked T, holding it up to her arm. It reached from her fingertips to her elbow. "That's one big bird!"

"*Trumpeter* swan," said Bernie, taking the feather from T. "This is so cool. Our tribe raised some trumpeters and donated them to the park. They released the flock last month. Trumpeters are native to Michigan. The nasty Mute swans, the ones with the orange bill that chase boaters are not—they are invasive, like the zebra mussels."

**Trumpeter Swan
(with a neck band)**

1/2 actual size!

69

"This is turning out to be a real scavenger hunt," I said, sketching the feather in my notebook. There was a rustling sound in the shrubs. It was that little striped beach bum again. He ran here and there near us. T was in love and cooed at it.

"Are you sure I can't give him just one peanut?" asked T. "He likes us. He keeps following us."

"Aunt Kitty said no," I reminded her. She looked crushed. "Well, maybe not by the house I guess."

"I think he wants us to follow him," said T looking much happier.

"Holy creeps! You're right!" I blurted and slapped my swollen forehead. "Micro-bear! Micro as in small and bear as in bear! Small bear. Bear cub! How did I miss that? He's hanging around because the bear cub in my dream wants us to help its mother. This micro-bear could be the bear cub taking us to help Misha-Makwa!" Sie stared at me.

"Holly, it's the allergy medicine talking. You can't be serious," she said. "Follow a chipmunk to find a ghost bear?"

"It's not the medicine. That wore off a long time ago," I said. "I don't think the micro-bear is really a cub and really taking us to Misha-Makwa. But I think it may tell us how to find the mother bear and what to do to help her."

"I'm up for adventure," said Bernie. "What can it hurt? Let's go, it'll be fun. Onward, Guardians! There's a lot to explore!"

Holy creeps, this Guardian was a real GeEK!

LAND OF THE GIANTS

We followed the micro-bear from the beach to the house, where it ran around to the back. It sat on the golf cart, watching us with its dark eyes.

"He's speaking to us!" I said. We ran to the cart and the wild-eyed rodent hopped down and eyed the trail, then ran back and forth across it.

"He wants us to follow him down the trail," I said. I looked at the cart. "Can you drive this thing, Bernie?"

"Dig it! Heck yeah," he grinned. "Auntie and I take these out all the time. Hop on guys, I know my way around this place like the back of my hand."

"This is fun," laughed T. "Follow that chipmunk!"

"Awesome!" Sie blurted. "Now were talking!"

"This is adventure, times ten!" I said. "We're following a little bear on the little bear island."

Bernie climbed behind the wheel and I sat in front, my hat turned around backwards. T perched like a homecoming queen on a crate in the back while Sie sat in the bed of the cart, her camera at the ready. We looked like one of those safari TV shows that chase wild animals. It was awesome.

We drove down the trail after the small, striped rodent. Every so often, the micro-bear stopped to wait for us to catch up and then ran on. We followed it further and further, until it climbed up to sit on a sign that read "Valley of Giants". There it eyed us, daring us to go on. Bernie stopped.

"Well, Team. Now what?" I asked. The skittering critter bounced down the trail and into the ferns.

"Rats, he's gone," cried T.

"Guardians, I think he wants us to go to the land of the giants," Bernie said thoughtfully. He flipped his goggles down on to his face and took a swig from his water bottle.

"Giants?" I asked. Ghosts, bears, aliens and now giants. This park held it all. Weirdness and fun times ten.

Tierra's

GORP Recipe!
almonds, M&Ms, peanuts, raisins, dried fruit, & more M&Ms

"The giants live in the cedar forest," Bernie answered. We looked at each other. T's stomach growled. She crammed gorp from her pocket into her mouth.

"When my supply is gone we'll have about 20 minutes," she warned us.

"Then what?" asked Bernie.

"She gets as cranky as a Mama bear," said Sie, "and we don't want to go there!"

We drove on past a sandy lake when the forest started to get thick. Eventually the trail narrowed, so we parked the golf cart and walked down a dark path among ferns, flowers and tall trees. It was very magical looking. I just hoped that the big, friendly giants would tell us where to find the mother bear, Misha-Makwa, so we could help her.

"This is where the giants live," said Bernie, looking up through the branches. Patches of sunlight sparkled here and there. Rotting logs had gardens of ferns and saplings growing on their backs. The tangled roots of fallen trees hid flowers in their shade. Huge cedars loomed before us. It was silent. Their massive trunks were covered with knots that looked like faces.

"Its like a fairy forest," T said, touching the tough bark.

"The trees look like totem poles," said Sie, snapping photos of the bark and ferns.

"They look like they were carved," I said. "It's like you can see faces in them. Maybe there's a bear hiding here on one of them." I ran from tree to tree. We all scoured the area, looking

VALLEY
of the
GIANTS!

for a clue, but didn't find anything.

"Face it Holly, there's nothing here but giant trees. That chipmunk steered us wrong. He took us on a wild micro-bear chase," said Sie.

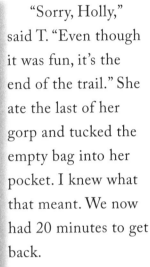

Cedar Giants!

"Sorry, Holly," said T. "Even though it was fun, it's the end of the trail." She ate the last of her gorp and tucked the empty bag into her pocket. I knew what that meant. We now had 20 minutes to get back.

"I was so sure we'd find a clue. There has to be a reason why it led us here," I moaned. I sat on the soft ground and pulled the claw-tifact out of my pocket, but I couldn't figure it out.

"I'm done," I said, scowling. "I'm done looking for clues. I was so sure we'd find something out here but there's nothing. Stupid rock!" I said, shoving it back into my pocket.

We started walking back down the trail to the cart. T's stomach growled right on cue. We now had 19 minutes to get back. Double rats.

AS LUCK WOULD HAVE IT

We all piled quietly back into the golf cart. Bernie slid his goggles down onto his face. I took one last look at the giant cedar forest.

"You know, Holly," said Sie, putting her hand on my shoulder, "you really have had pretty bad luck ever since you found that thing."

"I guess." I felt crushed, bottomed out, like I had stepped in a pile of steaming Hunter poo. Bernie started the cart and we rolled along. T's stomach grumbled every ten feet. I sighed about every twenty.

"Why are these trees so much bigger than the others, even the ones back on the mainland?" Sie asked Bernie.

"A long time ago men came here and cut down all the trees for lumber," Bernie explained. "But the winds off the water on this side of the island imbedded sand into the tree's bark. Over time, so much sand became imbedded that it made it impossible to cut these trees. The sand destroyed the lumbermen's saws."

"That's cool. Isn't it, Holly?" she poked me.

"Yeah. Sure. Cool," I mumbled. Just then there came a *clunka—thunka—clunk—thup—thup* sound from the back end of the cart.

"Um, what's that?" Sie asked Bernie.

"I don't know," he said and kept driving. But the thupping sound turned into a flapping sound. I leaned over the side of the golf cart.

"Guys, we have a flat tire," I said. Bernie stopped in the sandy road. He got out to inspect the tire.

"Yup, it's a flat alright," he said kicking at it. I went to look at it too.

"Flat? The tire is completely off the wheel thing," I said, bending over.

"Do you have a spare tire?" asked Sie, looking around.

"Uh, yeah," he said, grinning and shrugging. "Back at the park garage."

"But it's a long way back," whined T. Panic spilled out of her eyes like a two pound bag of M&Ms in a one pound bowl. "It's getting dark and I'm hungry."

"Well, I guess we can just drive on it the way it is," I

suggested. "Or we can try to put the tire back on." Bernie and Sie and I grunted and lifted and grunted while T shoved the tire back on the rim. Then we piled on the cart and cheered. It went another twenty feet before we heard thup-thupping again. We did this six times before we gave up and collapsed in the sandy road to rest. I was so hot and tired I felt like my freckles would pop right off my face.

"Now," panted Bernie, "we walk." We peeled ourselves off the ground and began walking. It reminded me of the movies where people are stranded in the desert after their camel fell over and there was no water and the sun was setting and they had a gazillion miles to go to get out of the desert—even though we only had a half a mile to go.

"The sky's getting all pinky-purple. It's way past dinner," said T, gripping her belly.

"What happened to all of your trail mix?" asked Sie.

"It's gone. Food—gone. Water—gone," she said weakly. "I picked out all the nuts to give to the micro-bear. He was so cute and hungry. He reminded me of my hamster Willy-Nilly-Wilma." She sighed. We all stared at her in disbelief.

"No wonder that rodent brought us out here, you kept feeding it," I said.

"Oh brother," said Sie, slapping her head. Bernie laughed. He pulled out the Smarties he found on the beach and offered one to T.

"Thanks," she said, shakily.

"That fat little micro-bear is probably back in camp right now telling all his friends," laughed Bernie.

We staggered along. "My feet hurt," sighed Sie.

"Well," I said. "We did get to see some really old giants." Then it hit me.

"That's it!" I yelled. "That's why we had to go to the Land of the Cedar Giants!" The Team looked at me, bewildered. "We had to go there for the story! Not just to hear it, but to see it in action and get to know it."

"What do you mean, Holly?" asked Sie.

"The story of the grains of sand saving the trees from the logger's saw. We are like grains of sand! If we all work together—not just us, but everyone who visits the park—we can help the Sleeping Bear's land and lakes!"

"Yeah," said Bernie. "Auntie Pearl did say that millions of people visited the park last year. Just think what kind of help those millions of "grains of sand" could be!"

HOW much Wind does iT taKe to MOVE sand?

- 7 - 8 m.p.h. slight movement
- 8 - 12 m.p.h. rolls fine sand
- 25 - 31 m.p.h. moves sand 1 mm.
- 39 - 46 m.p.h. "gale force", can lift sand 100' in the air

"And you mentioned the Sleeping Bear P.A.W. Beach Party Picnic on Saturday," I said, all re-energized now. "We could do something to tell the people about the lakes. Something that will get everyone's attention in a fun way."

"Yeah, but what?" asked T.

Just then we saw faint, bouncing lights ahead. It was like the desert mirage scene in the movies. Was it help or was it ghost aliens? At this point I really didn't care.

Then we could see a beat up, rusty green pickup rattling down the trail toward us. It was Aunt Kitty and Gram with Pearl standing up in the back. "We're rescued!" cried Sie.

"Kids, we were looking for you!" yelled Ranger Pearl. "Where's the cart?"

"Back there in the road," pointed Bernie. "We got a flat."

"No problemo," said Pearl, helping us up into the truck bed. "We'll pick it up tomorrow. Right now we'll get you tuckered troopers to HQ for some grub." We all squeezed into the bed of the truck, crammed in between buckets, shovels and rakes. It felt good to sit down, even if it was on a hard, lumpy tire.

We had a fun, bumpy drive back singing "The Bear Went Over the Mountain" and laughing as the sun set. We were all pretty exhausted and ready for dinner when we finally got back to the house.

That's when we found a surprise waiting for us.

SMARTER THAN THE AVERAGE BEAR

We opened the door into the kitchen and knew immediately that while we were out, our cottage had been invaded. Not by aliens, but by micro-bears. A hotdog bun bag that had been chewed and ripped was sitting on the floor in the middle of a pile of potato chips and oatmeal.

"Someone's been eating our oatmeal," said Sie, tip-toeing through the cinnamon-y oatmeal pile, "and left us quite a mess."

"My goodness! What a nightmare!" said Gram. "Didn't you kids put the food away?"

"I thought you did," Sie scowled at me.

"I did," I shrugged. "Most of it. Except for this stuff."

"Ow," said T, holding her gut.

"Looks like that smart chipmunk lead us to the cedar giants to distract us so he could come back and feed his family!" laughed Bernie. Gram got out a broom to sweep up the mess.

"There goes my dinner plans for Cinnamon-Oatmeal-Rolled-Pigs-in-a-Skillet casserole," sighed Aunt Kitty. Yikes. The sound of that recipe hurt even me. My possum gut can take only so much. I was kinda glad the little buggers got in.

"Change of plans," chuckled Pearl. "Hotdogs with beans for dinner and breakfast. At least the varmints haven't learned how to get into cans—yet." We went through the house doing a clean up, pick up.

"Someone got onto the bed and got into my pack," said T, looking inside her bag. "And they took my backup supply of trail mix."

"And someone chewed the stuffing from the chair!" yelled Sie, scratching her head.

"Um, does this story sound familiar, guys?" I asked, walking around the messy cottage.

"MiCRo BeArs"

"micro-terrors"
of house and camp--
but super-wicked cute!

"You mean Goldilocks and the Three Bears?" asked Bernie, finishing his pack of Smarties and flopping onto the couch.

"Sleeping bag in the water, flat tire, micro-bears ate our food," I said. "Gram did say this was a nightmare. I think Misha-Makwa is trying to tell us to pay attention again."

"Don't you get it, Holly?" said Sie. "You have had such bad luck since you found that stone. Which means we have *all* had bad luck. Maybe you should put that stone of yours back where you found it." She sighed and dropped, exhausted, onto a dining room chair. The leg snapped and she fell backwards onto the floor with a clattering crash.

"Coincidence?" Sie mumbled, as T helped her back up. "I call it bad luck."

I guess the chair was the last straw for Sie, because she marched to the kitchen. T was right behind her.

I didn't want to admit it. I didn't want to give up my awesome-times-ten claw-tifact.

"But, I think we're on the trail of the bear now," I said. "And I think she has more to say." I reached into my pocket to feel the stone's rough coolness.

"It's gone!" I squeaked. "I lost it." My heart pounded. I felt dizzy. The twins looked at me from the kitchen with their crossed arm, I-don't-believe-you-double-trouble-two-blurred-into-one-angry-best-friend look.

"Really, it is," I said, feeling sick

"Don't worry, Holly," said Bernie quietly. "It'll turn up."

"Yeah," I said, plopping onto my sleeping bag on the floor under the living room window, but I wasn't so sure. "I suppose I should get ready for a night of night-bear nightmares. Maybe I won't have them though, now that the stone is gone."

Aunt Kitty and the Team came out with plates of beans and franks for everyone. Things feel better when your belly is full. Pretty soon we were all laughing.

"You mentioned earlier," said Sie, "that what happened today was like Goldilocks and the three bears. I don't know how that fits in with your dream of the cub wanting you to find his mother, but it almost seems like a clue."

"Maybe Goldilocks is the name of the micro-bear," I said, yawning and trying to hold up my tired head. "It was one rude rodent. Maybe it took my claw-tifact, too."

"I guess we all had a part to play in that story. If I hadn't fed the chipmunk, none of this would've happened," said T. "So I don't think it was bad luck."

"Your stone didn't make bad stuff happen. Things just happened," said Bernie.

"Well, it could've been worse," I said. "Things could always be worse. It's funny what happened though, like a reverse version of the tale with the "bear" raiding the house and not Goldilocks." We chuckled and T grabbed her notebook and rainbow of glitter pens. I could see the Team was about to get to work. This looked like it might be an all-nighter. We scootched our sleeping bags closer together. Gram was snoring and the aunts were playing cards at the table.

"OK, let's look at the words," T said, chewing on the end of her glitter pen. "Micro-bear = small bear. In the story, the bears have a run in with Goldilocks. And actually, in the original version, it was not Mama, Papa and Baby Bear, but Big, Medium and Small Bear." The girl really knew her stuff. She's quite the expert on fairy tales. She wrote down every clue.

"But Goldilocks is a girl with golden hair, so who here is

Goldilocks?" asked Sie, pushing up her glasses.

"Maybe Goldilocks could mean a gold chain or padlock," suggested Bernie. T drew it all out.

"Well, all I know is that Goldilocks can't be me because I have red hair," I said. "So who is Goldilocks? I think that's the key clue here. If we find Goldilocks, we find the Mother Bear and can help her."

We sat there staring at the stars through the big window in the living room. In the distance a flash of lightning spread across the sky like a pink spider web.

"Come on Mama Bear," I said. "What are you trying to tell us?" By now the whole Team was sleeping while I sat in silence, watching the stars.

BiG Bear &
Little BeAr

ANGRY WATERS

This time, instead of waking up to the image of a floating gummy bear in my face it was Gram that I saw. But this time it was no dream.

"Holly, we have to pack. We're heading out."

"But I thought we were leaving tomorrow," I said groggily.

"There's a big storm on the way," said Pearl. "Storms on the big lake usually mean rough water for days and the boat might not run. If we don't leave now we could be stuck here for a while, and since the chipmunks raided the pantry, we wouldn't have enough food." Pearl's radio crackled from the kitchen. Scratchy voices mixed with static set a tone of gloom.

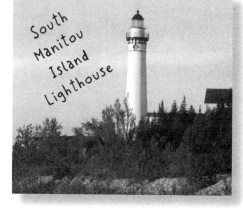

South Manitou Island Lighthouse

"They do have spare food at headquarters though," said T, and shrugged. "I checked on that."

I remembered the Beaver Island storm with the pelting hail and wind. Outside the window, Lake Michigan was already a steely gray, matching the sky above it. Aunt Kitty and Gram had the cooler and bags packed.

We rolled out of our sleeping bags and shared a couple of granola bars that the micro-bear had missed. A Park Service guy was outside with the golf carts waiting to load our gear.

"The waves look pretty rough today," said Sie as we carried out our cooler and loaded up our stuff.

"Yep, she sure looks angry," said Bernie. I hoped the lake wouldn't get too angry until we got back to the mainland.

When the boat arrived the captain and crew were hurried. No messing around today. I recognized tired hikers we had ridden across with the day before. Other hikers stayed on the island to weather the storm.

North Manitou Island

We sat in a huddle as the boat crossed the big lake. The white froth-tipped waves crashed into the back, spraying water up over the windows. The small boat rocked and rolled across the waves. One second all you could see was water, the next, nothing but sky.

"You really have to respect this big water," said Gram. "The Old Girl can be moody. She's pretty from a distance, but powerful." Waves crashed again into the back window of the boat. I saw where there was a crack in the rear window and wondered if the lake had done that. Everyone was quiet the whole trip back.

"This Manitou Passage used to be a super highway in shipping days," remarked Aunt Kitty. "As many as 150 boats have sunk here in the passage." There she goes again. Adding the creep factor, times ten. All I could think about was the cubs swimming that far, not making it across and being shipwreck number 151.

Reaching the mainland and stepping on solid ground never felt so good. We drove down the coast to Port Oneida and stopped at an overlook. The sky and water were now a deep, navy blue-black. The waves  were over ten feet high and the wind was so strong we could barely open the van door or stand outside.

"Gale force," shouted Ranger Pearl. "That means danger on the water." It was cool to see the many moods of the lake—from clear and calm like glass, to wavy and green, to dark, angry breakers. We were all pretty glad, times ten, to get back to the park farmhouse.

We ate a late lunch by the big stone fireplace and played Scrabble. The storm outside was distracting. Buckets of whipping rain slammed against the windows. Hunter kept looking at the door. I imagined the three bears and Goldilocks coming in for porridge.

"Hunter sure has been awfully whiny," I said.

"Maybe he doesn't like storms," T said and hugged Hunter. He looked up at her with big droopy eyes. "It'll be over soon fella," she crooned. The wind banged branches against the house and moaned. Lightning crackled and thunder shook the windows.

"Whoa, it's a good thing that we got back when we did," said Sie, looking outside.

I felt for my claw-tifact in my pocket and remembered that it was gone on its own journey. Rats.

"Maybe it was good that you lost that stone," T said. "You were having pretty bad luck."

Bernie played the word 'ivy' off of my word 'yikes'.

"Bad luck would be Ivy Buckthorn," I said pointing to his triple word play.

"That girl is one rude, unhappy camper," whistled Bernie, jotting down his score.

"Holy creeps!" I yelped. "That's it! Ivy Buckthorn has gold hair! Ivy Buckthorn is Goldilocks!" I jumped up, sending wooden letter tiles clattering across to the floor. Thunder boomed right on cue.

GOLDILOCKS, WHERE ART THOU?

Hunter barked. T and Sie stared at me openmouthed. My brain chugged like a steam engine. Thoughts were happening. Puzzle pieces were coming together like a Scrabble board. I felt dizzy from all of the clues linking.

"Your friend Ivy is Goldilocks?" asked Bernie. The Team and I stared at him.

"Uh, she's *not* our friend," said Sie, pushing up her glasses.

"Goldilocks! Of course!" T exclaimed. "Ivy Buckthorn has

yellow-gold hair. The cottage of the Three Bears is where Ivy Buckthorn is staying on Bass Lake, not the cottage on South Manitou." T ran to get her sketchbook with our clues.

"I don't know. This is creepy," said Sie, sitting down, taking it all in. Lightning flashed.

"And where there are Buckthorns," I said, "there is trouble, times three. I'll bet the answer is there somewhere, the thing that will help Misha-Makwa, the Sleeping Bear. We need to go back to the cottage to find out what that noise is."

"I was afraid you'd say that," said Sie.

"After what Buckthorn did on Beaver Island with the caiman and the theme park," I said, "I wouldn't put it past him to be raising bears or doing something horrible back there."

"What if they're home? We can't just knock on their door and say, 'Hello, what wrong and evil thing are you doing over here?'" said Sie. "We need a reason to go over so we can spy on them."

This was getting so exciting. I love it when pieces fall into place. We studied T's sketchbook. The pink drawings looked like the spidery web of lightning I saw last night. Everything connecting and all strands leading to the Buckthorns.

"So we need an excuse to go over there and look around," I said.

"Dig it!" blurted Bernie "We can invite her to the Sleeping Bear P.A.W. picnic."

"Naw," said Sie, "she knows we don't like her and it would look suspicious. Besides, we need a reason that will get us out of the boat."

"Hold on, guys, I've gotta use the ladies room," said T, running out of the room.

"That's it!" I hollered, jumping up. "We can say that T really, really has to use the bathroom! Ivy might be mean but hopefully she's not heartless."

"We need to go over there as soon as we can," said Sie. "We have to find out what's going on before the P.A.W. picnic."

"That means we have to do this tomorrow morning," I said.

T walked back into the room. "What'd I miss?" she asked, plopping onto the couch..

We all laughed. "We're using you for bait!" said Sie.

The next morning I woke up laughing, laughing at bouncing gummy bears. Like balloons, they floated about happily, in every size, shape and color, singing "The Teddy Bear Picnic" song. I was getting kind of used the chubby, puffy guys. T laughed, too, when I told her about the dream.

"Giant gummy bears," she said. "You're weird."

I got up and clipped my bear bells to my belt loop.

"Geez, Holly. I'll be so glad when this whole thing is over," said Sie. "I'm waiting for Piglet to arrive and take you to the One Hundred Acre Wood."

"Let's go girls," said Gram. "I still think it's odd that you want to fish in the lake where the Buckthorn cottage is. I thought you tried to avoid Ivy." Gram squinted at us, then slid her glasses down her nose to look me in the eye.

"The bass bite really good there," I said, looking away sideways and whistling through my teeth.

She chuckled. "Uh huh, something *is* up. Well, let's go."

I smiled at Gram with a big toothy grin and she rolled her eyes as we ran past her to the kitchen. We grabbed fruit and granola bars for breakfast on the road. We had a lot of work to do and just wanted to get this part done as quickly and as painlessly as possible. Like going to the dentist or taking a math test; if you do it and don't think about it, it goes fast.

We stopped by to pick up Bernie, who was excited to see us. We bounced down the bumpy, squishy road to Bass Lake. Gram had told Aunt Kitty that we were going back to Bass Lake and wanted to use the canoe.

"I can't wait to go fishing today," I said, looking in the rear view mirror. Gram was looking back at me. I smiled. "Good day to fish, Team. Hope we catch a big one."

"The rain should help get the water level back up a bit," said Aunt Kitty, as we pulled up to the lake. The sand was wet and Aunt Kitty pointed out otter tracks and mussel shells on the shore. Aunt Kitty had decided to enjoy the morning by the lake with Gram.

"Remember to stay in the shallows, kids," said Gram as we strapped on life jackets. "Even though the park canoe is wide and shouldn't tip, don't tempt it." She steadied the canoe as we stepped in. Bernie sat with a paddle in back and I grabbed one to sit in front. The twins sat in the middle. Gram shoved us off, still giving me a strange look.

"Ahem, your fishing pole, Holly," said Gram.

"Oh, yeah, thanks," I grinned. Sie winced and shook her head slowly.

"No wonder she suspects something," Sie whispered.

"Not too long, kids," Gram called.

"Don't worry," I yelled back. When I turned around I banged my face into the paddle and knocked my hat off. T snagged it before it hit the water. I could hear Gram sigh, even all the way out here.

SECRET MISSION: GOLDILOCKS

It was a bright, cool morning. I was hoping to see the otter who made the tracks on shore, but it was like all the animals had gone on vacation and we were alone on the lake. We stayed along the shore so no one could see our approach. We wanted to scope the place out to see if anyone was home. As we got closer to the cottage the growling, droning sound started up. I felt for my bear bells.

"We better hide in the weeds," said Bernie. Nearing the dock, we heard Ivy's high-pitched whine bounce across the water. The muffled growling sound stopped, car doors slammed and the engine roared. We heard the car pull away, then it suddenly got quiet.

"They must be gone," I whispered. We floated in the lily pads, waiting for the sound to start again. No one moved. Bull frogs bellowed, bees buzzed. Finally we edged the canoe towards the dock.

Just then Ivy stormed out of the house. Her face was red and angry and she looked like a bear about to charge. We all nearly jumped out of our skin and I dropped my paddle. When I reached for it the canoe rocked and T gave a little squeal. That's when Ivy noticed us, which made her face redder and madder.

"Squirrelberry Smellcake!" she screeched and stamped her

foot, narrowing her red eyes at us. "What are you doing here? What gives?"

"Um," I choked, "we just um wanted to tell you that um.... Fluffy likes his new home with Bernie." I said quickly, itching from head to toe. She made me so nervous I had completely forgotten our plan!

"Who's Fluffy?" she snarled.

"Your fish. The one you gave to Bernie," I said. "Fluffy's happy in his new home."

"Well, big whoop for Floppy," she said. "I hope he's happy. You can go now."

"Can we pull up to the dock and get out?" asked T. "I have to go to the bathroom." T's quick thinking impressed me. I never thought I would be so happy to hear those magic words.

Ivy crossed her arms and eyed us suspiciously.

"Why can't you just go in the woods?" she asked.

"Because...," T said and gestured towards Bernie.

"Oh fine. Come on in, but hurry it up." Bernie pulled the canoe up and held the dock as we all climbed out. Awesome times ten! Our plan worked! We would keep Ivy occupied while Bernie snooped around.

Ivy opened the squeaky screen door. The kitchen smelled like bacon mixed with a sickly, sweet rose-scented air freshener. Queenie growled from her plastic covered perch on a gawdy flowered couch.

"Knock it off, Queenster," Ivy said. "They're harmless." Ivy looked me up and down. "Yeah, harmless." She pointed the bathroom out to T.

"Hurry it up. My parents are gone to Traverse City. Doctor's appointment. They'll be back soon." Then she shot a look at Sie. "So what are you guys doing out here again anyway?"

"Uh, Holly was fishing," said Sie.

"Sie was taking pictures," I blurted at the same time. We stared at each other. Oops.

Ivy's eyes narrowed to slits.

"Which one is it?" she asked, her head cocked to one side. Queenie growled again from the couch.

"Well, uh, I was fishing while Sie was taking pictures," I stammered. Ivy raised her eyebrows, looking unconvinced. "Uh, pictures, uh for the, um, art show at the picnic...at the park... this weekend." I was sweating so bad my freckles were dripping. I looked at Sie who was staring at me in disbelief.

"Art show?" said Ivy, looking suddenly interested. "I didn't hear about an art show."

"Yeah, a trash art show," I blundered on. "Bernie makes the stuff all the time. Sells it, too. We're going back to the house today to work on our projects." Sie slapped her forehead.

"Trash? Sell it? Cool!" Ivy said, nodding. "So I'll come over to your place and do this art thing after lunch."

Holy creeps times ten! What did I just do?

"Oh, you don't have to do *that*," said Sie, looking panicked as T stepped out of the bathroom.

"But I don't have any art stuff," Ivy sneered. "My mom won't let me make a mess here so I'll make a mess at your house, so I can win this art show."

"What art show?" asked T as she walked up.

"Well, this has been *real* fun, but we should go," said Sie, grabbing T and me by the arm and turning us towards the door.

"Wait. What's the prize?" Ivy asked. "You never said how much I would win. I'm not going to waste my time if the prize isn't cash." She put her hands on her hips.

"Fifty dollars or a hundred," I blurted again. Sie pinched my arm. "Ow! I can't remember the exact amount. Fifty dollars I think. Yeah. Fifty. Maybe a hundred. A hundred. For sure," I stammered. Fire was shooting from Sie's eyes as she glared hotly at me.

"I'm a material girl," Ivy said. "Deal. I'll be there with bells on. You freaks are dumb, but you're kinda alright."

OPERATION IVY

Sie dragged me by my shirt out the door and T followed. Bernie, who was peering through the shed's dusty window, jumped when the screen door slammed. Ivy's head whipped around, her ponytail slicing the air.

"What are you doing over there?" she snapped, marching over to the rickety shed with a padlocked door.

"Um...nature call?" Bernie said, pointing towards the trees behind the shed. "You told Tierra to use the woods. So I did," he grinned.

Ivy's eyes were knife slits as she glared hard at Bernie.

Next to the shed was a pile of hoses, tires and garbage covered in overgrown weeds. On the door a sloppily-printed sign read: Absolootly NO Tresspassing! This Meens YOU! Do KNOT Nter!

"Do not enter," Sie read aloud. Ivy's head snapped back around at Sierra.

"The sign on the shed, 'absolutely' is spelled wrong," said Sie, pointing at the door.

"What's in there that 'absolutely no one' is allowed to see?" I asked. We must have been making Ivy nervous because she chewed on her ponytail. I never saw her do that before. She actually seemed to be sweating. Her eyes darted left and right like a pinball machine.

"It's Daddy's shed," said Ivy, trying to look casual. "There's dangerous stuff in it, garbage, poison. The usual. No big whoop. Here, I'll show you." She grinned a poky-toothed grin.

She pulled the key from her pocket and unlocked the chain on the door. The hinges squealed as it opened. The shed was dark and smelled bad. A red gas can sat in an oil stain on the floor, paint cans were stacked and dripping. A ratty-patched

tarp covered a bulky piece of leaking machinery; bags of bottles and boxes of trash were piled high. Poisons, buckets of junk, rusted wire fencing and sharp tools were crammed in the corners. No wonder no one was allowed inside. It looked like a toxic torture chamber, just a normal shed for the Buckthorns. And here I was, so sure we were really on to something.

"Mother says deadly things have to be locked up from now on. Poisons, dangerous tools, stuff," Ivy said, the wicked gleam leaving her eyes. "Now that there is a baby on the way." Her shoulders sagged, her ponytail drooped.

The Team and I looked at each other. Baby? Holy creeps! Another Buckthorn?!

"That's where my parents are today," Ivy said, kicking the ground with her toe. "Stupid baby doctor appointment." She went from cheery talking about deadly things to sad talking about a baby. Somehow I think it should have been the other way around, but this was Ivy, after all.

"Parents are so selfish," she grunted. "Why do they need another kid when they have me?" She kicked the shed door shut and locked it. The Team and I were still standing there in shock.

"But having a baby is awesome, Ivy," said T. "That's usually a good thing."

"No, it isn't. My parents—won't love me anymore," Ivy whined. "I won't get as much, they won't have time for me, I won't be as important. I can't compete with a stupid, wiggly fat baby. I'll be forgotten. Even worse, the kid gets my room at home and I get the downstairs level."

"Well, we should be getting back," Bernie said. We started walking towards the dock. I looked back at Ivy standing alone by the shed.

"Don't worry, Ivy, it will—oof!" Sie's foot flew out in front of me. I went head first into a jungle of ferns and blackberry vines. She glared at me, then helped me up, my bear bells tangled and jingling as I got to

my knees. I found a crumpled piece of paper on the ground and pocketed it as I got up. I guess Sie figured that I'd said enough and was trying to shut me up, so I decided to zip my lip before I

got any other bruises. But then T picked up where I'd left off.

"Just because the baby is new," said T, "they won't forget about you. You get to be a big sister."

"True," Ivy sniffed, tagging along behind us. Then she looked up. "I'm not crying. A stupid mosquito—flew up my nose." She honked into a Kleenex. The sound reminded me of a foghorn.

"I guess I can boss the kid around and it can be my servant. It certainly can't be cuter than me. Maybe it might be OK. But I'm still mad that they did this to me. Maybe they'll let me name it."

"Yeah, there you go Ivy," said T. "That's the spirit."

Sie rolled her eyes and shoved us into the canoe.

"Maybe I can name the kid Catastrophic or Potbelly. I like Potbelly. Has a nice ring to it," Ivy brightened. "I do feel better," she said and laughed a kind of odd snarly, snorty laugh. I cringed. She sounded like she doesn't practice laughing much.

"What time should I be at your place Squishface—Shortstuff—er—Halley?" Ivy called from the dock. I didn't answer. T poked me in the ribs.

"Um, one o'clock today?" I croaked.

"Super, Smellburst." Her ponytail whipped and cracked like its old self as she marched back towards the house. We paddled away quickly.

"This doesn't mean we're friends, you know," she yelled to us. We heard the door squeal and slam shut as her evil laugh bounced across the lake like a demented loon.

HOOKING THE BIG ONE

Sie moaned and collapsed in the bottom of the canoe. Bernie paddled from the rear. T sat quietly, fiddling with her hair, while I sat in the front, gripping my paddle.

"What...just...happened...?" I asked no one in particular. For a moment the only sound was water dripping from Bernie's paddle. Then Sie lifted her head. I could feel her laser eyes burning through my hat into the back of my skull.

"*YOU* happened, Holly," Sie growled through gritted teeth as she sat up. "You opened your big mouth and now Ivy, our Arch Enemy, is coming over, TO-DAY, to make art for a show that doesn't exist, to win money that we DON'T HAVE!" I cringed.

"You keep mentioning an art show," T said. "What art show?"

I slowly twisted around on my seat, and explained to T and Bernie what had happened in the cottage. Then I tried to give Sie my best smile.

"Don't," said Sie, pointing at me. "YOU need to figure out what you're going to do."

"OK," I whispered, and turned back around, not wanting to get poked in the eye. My brain buzzed, my skin crawled with blackberry scrapes and renewed sunburn, my freckles quivered in embarrassment. Then Bernie cleared his throat.

"Well," he said, shrugging. "There's not much we can do. We can't keep Ivy from coming over, so let's make art! We can still put on an art show—I'll talk to my Auntie Pearl and tell her we came up with the idea to do something special at the P.A.W. picnic. I think she'll love it."

I turned around and beamed at Bernie.

"Yeah!" I cried, my voice bouncing across the water. A kingfisher leapt from a cedar, cackling in protest as it flew away. "The art we make with trash can teach people about things that can hurt the park! And just like the million grains of sand, we can protect the park and the water if we all work together!" Thanks to Bernie I went from feeling like a tiny water flea to the eagle we'd seen the other day with its fish prize!

Sie sighed loudly. "Fine," she said and slumped back down.

"Oh hey, speaking of water," chirped Tierra, "did anybody find any clues about the what's happening to the lake? The only thing I noticed was the rainbow painted shed and weed poison cans. Yikes."

"The shed sign seemed weird," said Sie, picking herself up off the bottom of the boat again. "But then they have signs all over their place at home. How about you, Bernie, did you find anything?"

"Just a bunch of old hoses," he said. "I wish we'd heard that noise again while we were there. I'm sure it's coming from behind their cottage, but we still don't know what it is."

"I never would have thought of the Buckthorns as recycling people," I said. "The shed was full of bottles and garbage."

"Some people collect things," said T. "Our aunt in Florida has kept the caps of every milk jug she ever opened."

"Well, we got a way better look than I thought we would," said Bernie.

"I wonder what was under that tarp," I said, shaking my head. None of us seemed to be thinking clearly with the misery of a day with Ivy hanging over us. "Maybe we can pick Ivy's brain when she comes over."

"That shouldn't take too long," Sie snorted.

We paddled up to shore. I must have really looked like a mess, because as we got closer I could hear Aunt Kitty gasp.

"Oh my, Holly!" she said, looking at me and clapping her hand over her mouth.

"Catch anything?" Gram asked, smirking, as she pulled the canoe ashore.

"Oh, we snagged a big one," Sie said, glancing at me.

"From the looks of you, Holly, it's more like *it* snagged *you*," chuckled Gram.

ART DAY WITH IVY

On the way back to the Crouch Farm we told Gram and Aunt Kitty about our "idea" for a trash art show. They were super geeked. Bernie called his Aunt Pearl to ask her if we could put together an art show at the P.A.W. Picnic. Bernie was grinning as he hung up the phone.

"Let's gather trash, Guardians!" he said. "The show is a go! Auntie Pearl wants us to make signs about the show. But it's a no go on the cash prize. She said they can give the winner a Sleeping Bear Dunes t-shirt instead."

"Well, I guess we don't have to tell Ivy that," I shrugged.

"But she's gonna find out!" Sie insisted.

"At least she won't find out until after the show," I said.

We watched the clock. It was almost one and Ivy would be here soon. Then we saw the Buckthorn's white SUV barreling down the road. Gravel sprayed across the lawn as they whipped into the driveway.

Sie and I sighed. It had already been a long day and it was about to get longer with Ivy around.

"Just be yourself," whispered Sie. "Don't be creepy. Oh, and sorry about all that," she added, pointing to my Band-Aid covered knees, and calamine lotion coated scratches. I took the ice from my head. I had forgotten sunscreen again and I'd gotten my sunburn sunburned while we were out. The way I felt it probably would have been easier to wrassle a bear.

Bernie, T, Sie and I stood at the door and took a deep breath. Ivy stepped inside. The door slammed.

"What gives gang? Long time no smell," she snorted. "So where's the art stuff?"

"First, we're going to make signs to tell people about the art show," explained T. "We need to show them that the lakes need people to help protect them and keep them healthy for their kids and grandkids." Ivy looked at me.

"What happened to you, Smudgepot?" she snorted. "Run into a train?" I looked at Sie. "Don't talk much, do ya?"

Bernie stepped in. "Let's get started!" he said cheerfully.

"Awesome," I breathed a sigh of relief. This mission was far more dangerous than when my Wild women relatives had encountered wild animals and I was happy to have the team behind me.

"We are working together to bring good stuff to the lakes," I said. "Huron, Ontario, Michigan, Erie and Superior. Ranger Pearl calls that 'H.O.M.E.S. land security'. And just like the sand embedded in the cedar tree bark that forms a protective armor, if we get more people to help, it will be like how the sand protected the trees. There is power in numbers. Team Wild + Team Ivy = Team work. Times two." I tried to smile.

Ivy looked at me like she'd just stepped in a steaming pile of Queenie poo.

"I don't know what you're talking about and don't really care," Ivy snorted. "I didn't come here to make a stupid poster. I came here to make art to win the contest." Ivy crossed her arms and tapped her foot impatiently.

"Fine," said T. "Then I guess I'm gonna have the best poster." She sat down at the table and started drawing with her fruity-scented, glitter pens.

Ivy watched over T's shoulder for a minute, one eyebrow slightly raised.

"Well, it's not fair that everyone will be looking at *your* artwork," Ivy said, sitting down next to T. "Point me to the markers, Shortstuff, I'm doing a poster too."

"The posters should tell people not to litter the beach, and to help clean it up," said Sie.

"And about how important a clean lake is," said Bernie.

Scissors snipped and glue dripped while the smells of squeaking grape and orange scented markers filled the air. Pretty soon Hunter came in the kitchen whimpering.

"I'm with you, Huntie. Snack time!" Sie grabbed a dog biscuit the size of her shoe and tossed it to him. I got up and stretched my sore body.

"I made one with a loon singing a sad song," said T, nibbling on a graham cracker.

"Nice work," said Ivy nodding in approval, "but lame, predictable." She crammed two crackers almost into her mouth. Crumbs covered

the floor as she held up her piece. "I however, made a zombie turtle choking on a birthday party balloon and attacking people for revenge in its final death throes. Now *that* will really grab people's attention."

Holy creeps! T looked horrified. I have to admit though that it did get the message across rather well.

"Um, wow Ivy," said Sie. "That's um—intense."

"Yeah, thanks," she smiled a strange twisted smile. It seemed like some new weird facial contortion her face was trying to work out.

"Maybe I should do something like this for my art entry. If my zombie turtle can impress you bozos, then my art will wow the judges. I'm certain to win this time." Sie gave me a look.

"Ah, yeah, sure," I said, and flashed her a big toothy grin.

"If you smile at me like that again, Shortstop," Ivy said, "You'll need more band-aids."

CREATIVE CRAFTING, TIMES TWO

We moved outside to the picnic table to work on our art projects while the posters dried inside. Tierra fashioned a shorebird out of a diet cola bottle with long pipe cleaner stick legs. Sierra made a bird with plastic spoon feet and a spoonbill. Bernie, still geeked from finding the Trumpeter swan feather on South Manitou Island, made a long Styrofoam cup-necked swan attached to a one-gallon milk jug. Ivy was working on fish from two liter bottles which I must say were kinda cool with their jagged sharp teeth.

I couldn't think of what to make, but now that there really was a prize, even if it was only a T-shirt, I wanted to win.

I needed to think big. Something spectacular.

Then it hit me.

Fossils. Ancient. Big. I ran out back behind the garage. A softish, half-rotted log as tall as me that Hunter had been chewing on would now become my "log sturgeon". I gave it bottle cap eyes and paper plate fins. We had some craft paint but not enough to complete my masterpiece.

I went inside to look

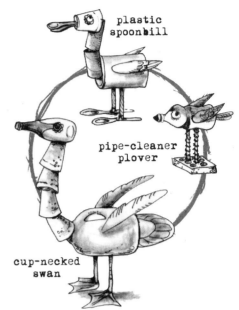

plastic spoonbill

pipe-cleaner plover

cup-necked swan

Make TRASH ART out of litter!

around the kitchen. I was in luck! Aunt Kitty's stash of raspberry gelatin! That'll work. I remembered Mom using that stuff to dye baskets for a craft show. The red color would make my sturgeon stand out.

I used the microwave to heat water and dissolve the mix. Now I needed something to carve the log with. Mom wouldn't let me have a real knife yet, probably due to the fact that I spent a lot of time on the ground. If I had my claw-tifact, that would have done the job. Instead I used a plastic fast food knife. It would have to do. I was loaded up, balancing bowls to head out the door when I called to Gram upstairs.

"Gram, can I use some jello for an art project?" I waited for her answer. It was her yoga time.

"Sure Holly. Aunt Kitty bought it to make her famous Seven

Layer Lavender-Pineapple-Potato-Peanut-Jello Salad, but in the name of art, please use it."

I carried everything out to the back of the garage. I didn't want anyone to see it just yet. I wanted it to be a surprise. I propped up the log and rounded its head over with the serrated knife. The wood was so soft it cut like butter.

Then I painted its long log body with the gelatinous paint mix. I slathered it on trying to be careful around my paper plate fins. But the goo ran down the sides of my fish, creating a red raspberry puddle on the ground, so I needed more.

I went back inside and took the rest of the jello boxes, about six, to make another big batch. I cooked that up and took it out to finish painting my fish. It was looking pretty good and pretty red. It would take a day to dry but it wasn't bad. Actually, it was pretty darned amazing. I was sure to win the Sleeping Bear P.A.W. trash art contest.

I was picking up my tools when I realized that I had stepped in the puddle of red runoff. Sand and grass stuck to my boot. I kicked sand over the puddle. In case it rained, I decided to put my sturgeon in the garage to keep it dry. So I dragged it through the door and propped it up in the corner. By now some sturgeon log tail bits were chunking off. I collected those and smushed them into place hoping it would hold. I had used all the "paint" so repair work wasn't going to happen. I hoped it would be dry by Saturday. I looked at it one more time and smiled, then closed the door and turned—to run right smack into Sie.

"Geez, Holly. You're a mess. What have you been doing? Where've you been? I've had to baby sit Ivy this whole time." She looked frazzled.

"It's a surprise. I am planning an unveiling of it at the picnic. All I can say is that it's cool, times ten."

"I can't wait to see it. It must be colorful," said Sie, eyeing my red-stained hands and boots.

"Has Ivy said anything about what her dad's up to?" I asked.

"Not yet," sighed Sie. "Everything *but* that."

Back at the picnic table Ivy and T were putting finishing touches on their projects. T looked like she was in pain since Ivy was gabbing nonstop. Bernie must have gone inside. I was beginning to wonder when Ivy would go home.

Two-liter Tiger Muskie with "food chain"

"Clean up and wash up for dinner kids!" Gram called from the back porch. Oh, great, she had invited Ivy to dinner! The Team and I sighed. I had to change and wash up before Gram saw me, so I went in the front door. When I was done everyone was gathered in the dining room.

"So what do you call this stuff Mrs. Wild? It looks like weeds," asked Ivy.

"It's called *salad*," answered Gram, raising an eyebrow. "It has dried cherries, fresh strawberries and walnuts tossed with lettuce and spring greens."

"Doncha have gravy to put on it? That's what I usually eat." She grinned with a sprig of green poking out the corner of her mouth. "Eew, weeds!" Ivy whined and spit it out onto her plate.

"I'll bet you'd enjoy Piping plover drumsticks," joked Sie.

"Sounds good, I love piping hot spicy stuff," Ivy said, picking the berries out of her salad. "This stuff is like poor people food, not like what I'm used to eating. And we'll be eating even better after Daddy gets rich. He's going to be richer than the thing on Beaver Island rich. He's been working on this plan since March. There's going to be a big surprise at the beach party on Saturday and Daddy says I get be Miss Buckthorn Brew and ride on the float."

My freckles started tingling and I noticed the Team picked up on it too. Was Ivy about to spill the beans?

"Well, what kind of surprise," I asked, trying not to look too interested. Ivy stiffened.

"Well, um, it's not *that* big of a surprise," she said, suddenly looking uncomfortable, her eyes darting around the table. "Daddy doesn't want me to say anything. Besides, it's none of your beeswax." She bit down on a cherry tomato, squirting seeds across the table, then she belched loudly. "OK, I think I'm done eating now."

That was Gram's cue. She jumped up from the table and ran to the phone to call the Buckthorns to come get Ivy. "Too bad you can't stay for dessert!" she called over her shoulder.

After Ivy left we all collapsed in a heap.

Yes, I believe wrassling a bear would've been easier and much less painful.

THE STUPOR NATURAL

Gram was not happy with my sunburn being worse. It hurt wearing my clothes. So Aunt Kitty ran to the store for aloe and Popsicles. When she got back I got slathered in green goo and put to bed in one of Gram's Detroit Tiger t-shirts.

"Well, we got a few more clues," said T, eating a grape Popsicle. "I took down notes after Ivy left. Buckthorn Brew sounds suspicious."

"Yeah, we can go over them tomorrow," said Sie. "Right now Holly looks like a gooey gummy bear. You really need to rest. Sorry about the rough day." She looked really sad.

"It's OK, you had to do what you had to do," I slurred. "I just hope we can find out what Goldilocks is up to." Then my head hit the pillow and I was out.

I wasn't asleep long when I heard a clang and then a soft grinding sound outside the window. I thought maybe Aunt Kitty had gone out to the van for something. Then I heard footsteps in the kitchen. Hunter

started whimpering upstairs. I hoped no one was messing around with my log sturgeon. I didn't trust Ivy and I wouldn't put it past her to sabotage our projects so she could win. Then the sound got closer. Closer, as in the bathroom that leads to our bedroom closer!

"Guys," I whispered, hoarsely. The Team was out cold. A day with Ivy was like a day with a wild boar. The sound of footsteps entered the room. I covered my head. I heard breathing near me. I could feel a presence. The air was as thick as the jello I had painted on my log fish.

I squeezed my eyes shut. The thing stopped right next to my bed and paused, then it took another step. When it did the smoke alarm in the living room went off.

"Ahhhhhh!" I yelled, hitting the floor running. I ran with my

flashlight through the kitchen to the stairs and yelled for Gram. Hunter barreled past, baying, and nearly knocked me over. I ran through the living room and back into our bedroom.

"Ghost!" I screamed, running through the bedroom flailing my arms in my dazzle and stun mode and waving my flashlight. The twins sat up in terror and pointed at me.

"Zombie!" Sie shrieked.

"Alien!" T bellowed. I wailed again, thinking they saw it behind me and jumped onto my bed. Hunter was in the kitchen barking at the smoke alarm. Gram threw open the door, flipped on the light and bolted into our room.

"Are you girls OK?" Gram asked, bewildered and out of breath. I was sitting up with my sleeping bag pulled up to my neck and my flashlight on. Aunt Kitty had stopped the alarm and was going through the house room by room and gave an all clear. The twins blinked at me bleary-eyed.

"Holy Toledo! *What* is going on?" Gram said, sitting on my bed. "This is not the time to be holding a fire drill, Holly."

"I-I heard a ghost," I trembled. Then I thought about it. "Awesome, that's the first ghost I've ever seen, except I had my eyes closed and my sleeping bag over my head."

"I thought you were a flailing zombie," said Sie, reaching for her glasses.

"I thought you were an alien floating in your white shirt and flashing light," said T. "She's been having lots of bear nightmares lately," T explained to Gram as Aunt Kitty came in and sat on my bed.

"Nightmares? Bears? Why didn't you tell us, Holly?" asked Gram hugging me gently.

"Well, the Team and I were working on it," I said shyly. "I was trying to figure things out on my own. I started having bear dreams as soon as we got to the park. After I found this rock they got weirder. Then I lost the rock. But this wasn't a dream this time, this was a real ghost. It made the smoke alarm go off." The twins shivered.

"Sounds like someone wants to get your attention," Gram said, patting my leg.

"It sounds to me like she's been called by Misha-Makwa," said Aunt Kitty, "the Great Bear of legend, the Mother Bear of the Ghost Forest."

"As you know, bears are the number one fear of Wild women," I said.

"Oh, I wouldn't say that dear," said Aunt Kitty. "Sure, we've had our run-ins with them, but there are bigger things out there than bears to fear. Bears gave us good practice for the really big things we might face one day."

"I guess so," I said, thinking for a moment. Then I sat up straight. "I will face my fears. After the sturgeon release I am camping outside with the help of my Team and speaking to Misha-Makwa myself!" I grinned at the wide-eyed twins.

"You're going to overcome your fear of bears with us?" asked T, gulping.

"Not just my fear of bears, but my fear of the dark, too," I said proudly. "Team, we're going to rough it. Camping for real in a tent under the Big Dipper, not in a house under a window."

"Sounds like a plan," yawned Aunt Kitty. "Every Wild woman has had to do it sooner or later—camp under the stars."

"It won't be so bad, guys, we have Hunter here to protect us," I said. "It's settled. Camp out on Sturgeon Release Day. Tomorrow I conquer my fears." Gram and Aunt Kitty got up and shuffled out towards the door.

"But w-what about the foot steps? The smoke alarm?" asked Sie, quivering.

"Oh, that?" Aunt Kitty said, shrugging as she closed the door. "That was just a ghost."

MIGHTY BRAVE

After the night of unusual events I slept like a pink claw-shaped rock—wherever it was sleeping these days. I woke up feeling so much better that I felt like having a big, buttery waffle with maple syrup. Maybe two. I hopped out of bed to get dressed. Today was Sturgeon Release Day.

"You're up early," yawned Sie. "No more weird dreams or ghostly visits?"

"Nope," I said walking into the bathroom. "I'm good to go and ready to rumble." I heard the girls giggle in the next room as I washed carefully and dressed.

"What's so funny?" I called. Sie snickered.

"T thinks you like Bernie. That's why you're being all brave and camping out," Sie said. "Among other things." My freckles sizzled beneath the green aloe bits that still clung to my face. I opened the door.

"What other things?" I demanded. I stood, hands on my hips, my hair poking out all over like a hedgehog. Combing my sunburned head was out of the question. This was a hat day.

"It's OK, Holly," said T. "It's cute. The two of you are a lot alike." My face felt hotter than when it was fried to sunburned crisp. Then the two girls threw pillows at me and giggled.

"I'm mighty!" I said, strapping on my mini-explorer kit and

walking into the kitchen. "I'm facing my fears and camping out. And I am having waffles." I knew that would get T up and out of bed.

After a breakfast of two and a half waffles and Gram and Aunt Kitty trying to clean the aloe out of my hair, we left for the Manistee River to meet Bernie. Hunter sat in the rear of the van and kept his head between ours. He'd been lonely and not liking being chained up at the farmhouse. Chewing the front steps from boredom had become his pastime. Aunt Kitty worried he would chew the whole front porch off, so going for a little drive did the old fella some good.

It was a winding drive past the park boundary to the Manistee River. Cars, trucks and vans were parked all over the edges of the road. People of all ages milled about, crowding around a small trailer beneath towering pines where a generator was running. Little kids ran around the trailer chasing each other. Everyone was having a good time.

"Hey, that sounds like the motor noise we heard by Ivy's place," I said. "I wonder if that's what is in Buckthorn's shed."

"What would the generator be running?" asked Sie. "Maybe that's what is under that big tarp."

Just then Bernie pushed his way through the crowd. Nearby Ranger Pearl and some folks in uniform stood with Odawa tribal members.

"So where's your fossil fish, Bernie?" I asked. The girls shot a big grin at me. I ignored them.

"In here," he said motioning to the trailer, "in the 'Sturgeon Station'". He lead us into the trailer where we looked into metal tubs where water bubbled and gurgled.

Inside the tanks several tannish-gray spotted fish the size of Gram's shoe were swimming about. They had long, pointy, flatish noses with scaly plates on their back.

"Here he is. Stumpy! I raised him from a small fry, when he was only as big as a dime," he said, proudly pointing to the fish without a tail swimming in one of the tanks. "I fed him brine shrimp when he was a youngster and then blood worms when he got bigger."

"So you're Nahma, the sturgeon, the spirit of the lake," I said, admiring the dinosaur-like fish.

"Nahma is the king of fish. They've been around for millions of years. Hopefully after today they'll be around for millions more," said Bernie.

"But if he has no tail, will he be OK?" T asked.

"There's a place for everyone in the tribe," grinned Pearl, as she entered the trailer. "Everyone has a job to do—live their own life." The fish circled around the tank. "Besides, he's got to be free. It's no life being cooped up in a tank all the time. Especially when they can grow up to eight feet long!"

"Holy creeps, that's big," I said. The twins peeked at the other tanks.

"When we release them into the river today, they'll be on their own in a new home. But they do have radio transmitters imbedded in their skin so we can check on them," said Bernie.

Outside, elders and children, aunties and uncles, gathered in a circle around a table.

"It's time for the ceremony!" said Bernie. We

moved to a clearing under some pines. A beautiful beaded bag, a braid of sweet smelling grasses and herbs were laid out on the blanket-covered table.

"Welcome," a tribal elder boomed. "Today we celebrate a journey, a moving out of good things into the world. The U.S. Forestry folk and the Odawa people have worked hard together to help this fish return to these life-giving waters. Together is a good way to make sure good things get done right. I'm happy that you all can be a part of it. Thank you, Megwetch."

Then a young boy helped the elder perform a special ceremony. Singing softly, the elder held the pipe to the four winds. That, mixed with the rising smoke and the music of the pines nodding over our heads, was a beautiful moment. Then all became silent and thoughtful. It was a time to think about journeys. A parade of people walked out of the trailer with the buckets of fish. That's when the cheering began.

Helpers in uniform and tribal folk alike carried the fish to the banks of the Manistee River. Kids ran laughing to the shore. Elders smiled as groups gathered around their fish. Each adult gently picked up a sturgeon for the children to see and touch. A few even sent them off with goodbye kisses.

"Here come the Grandfathers," children called to the river.

Fishing boats drifted by. A fisherman standing on the bank who had just caught a huge red and brown trout watched us. I hoped these little Nahma would have a chance with all of the boat motors in the river, not to mention hungry eagles, kingfishers, herons and fishermen!

Bernie picked up Stumpy and gave him a kiss, "Megwetch," he said to his squirming tailless fossil friend and placed him in the water.

"It's hard to see a friend go on his way," said Gram. "But it's good to be there to wish him well." Then Gram and Aunt Kitty and the Team and I stood with Bernie

and watched Stumpy take his first steps into the wild.

The fish sat there for a moment. There was a tear in Bernie's eye as his challenged friend began to swim away. Ranger Pearl gave him a squeeze.

"You did a good job raising him," Sie said, sniffing. Bernie watched the little fish in the shallows. Then it wiggled its tailless body and disappeared into the river.

"Do you think they're scared?" asked T. "Or do you think they're excited to see new places?"

"I think both," said Aunt Kitty, dabbing her eyes. "They'll learn. Like us, they have a long way to go and a long life ahead. They'll come back here to spawn when they are mature."

"As Eleanor Roosevelt once said, 'Do one thing every day that scares you,'" said Ranger Pearl, her thumbs in her belt.

"Dig it! This is Stumpy's big day," said Bernie, giving us each a high five. "Let's celebrate."

"Mine too," I said. "We both get to head out into the wild. I'm camping out tonight, to face my fears of the dark."

Bernie grinned at me. "That is big," he said.

Around us people were thanking the grandfather sturgeon for returning to the waters and wished them well on their journey. Then Aunt Kitty walked up to us with a bucket. Ranger Pearl handed me a sturgeon to hold.

"Holy creeps! They are so weird looking and weirder feeling—kinda rubbery." I smiled at the speckled gray fish. It did look like an alien! "I name you Specks. Go look for Stumpy and be his friend. He needs one."

"Teamwork," said Sie, as she and T touched its smooth back.

"Goodbye, little guy. Grow big and strong." The three of us placed Specks into the water. It wiggled off a ways, gliding over stones with its large fins like it was flying. Then, zip! Off it went into the deeper part of the river. The four of us kids with Ranger Pearl, Gram and Aunt Kitty watched the water.

"Awesome, times ten," I said.

Right then I knew I could camp out. If Stumpy could go off into the wild, so could I.

WILD CAMPOUT

"Tomorrow is the Sleeping Bear P.A.W. Beach Party Picnic," said Gram. "A grand finale ending to the Park Adoption Week for volunteers and visitors. Are you girls ready?" she asked as we pulled into the farmhouse driveway.

"Yep, we sure are. Our signs, our art, everything," I said. My art! I had to make sure it was dry. I ran out to the garage and pulled it into the sun. It was still tacky. After just seeing a real sturgeon my sculpture seemed to look more like a big red log with eyes. Or a giant raspberry fruit roll up. I wiped my hands on my shorts and inside my hoodie pockets. Then I noticed I had stepped in the red puddle of sand, jello and leaves again. Holy creeps. I hoped the log would be dry in the morning.

Log StuRgEon

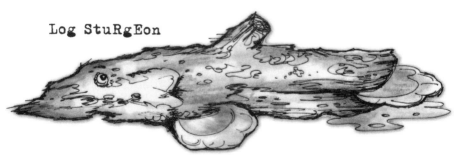

After an outdoor dinner of chicken sausages and beans and rice at the picnic table, I went and moved my log sturgeon back into the garage for the night. It had dried some more and would be perfect by morning. I was sure, times ten, that my fossil log fish would be a hit.

"So campers, let's get that tent set up for tonight," said Aunt Kitty, her eyes twinkling. "You can use mine. It's very roomy. It has to be if it accommodates Hunter," she giggled. Oh, great, yet another place for me to spend hours in a dog drool and hair covered place. Pretending it was wolf hair and wolverine spit instead made me feel better.

After we cleared away the plates and washed dishes, Gram and Aunt Kitty pulled out the tent. Picking out the actual camping spot in the yard was the longest part of the set-up phase. It took about half an hour because it had to be far enough away for me to feel 'wild' yet close enough to the house for T to run to the bathroom. And not too close to the halogen garage light and keep Sie awake all night but close enough to the dim porch light for us to sleep.

At long last, the final pole was snapped into place and we ran to get our gear and make it "home" for the night. I tossed my sleeping bag and my hoodie inside on the ground for a pillow. Done!

I turned around to find T dragging an air mattress behind her and a bundle of clothes.

"I have essentials for camping comfort," she said, pushing and shoving the mattress through the tent door like a limp, hot pink manatee.

Then out came Sie carrying a folded cot. There was much banging, bumping and thrashing going on inside as she unfolded it. It looked like they were on a teeter-totter with the two of them each sitting on an end to open it. Then T pulled out a battery-operated pump to blow up her bouncy air mattress.

When it was safe to enter, I crawled inside and found my way over to my little bag and pillow. The sky was getting all purpley-pink and darkish dusk. The full moon rose over the farmhouse. We heard steps outside the screen door.

"Sleeping out under the stars," said Gram. "You're wild women now. But we'll keep the porch door open for you. Hunter is just inside."

"Thanks, Gram," I said fluffing up my hoodie pillow. As she zipped up the tent I really wished I had my lucky bear claw-tifact. But I did have my handy flashlight—with fresh batteries. Gram went back inside and the tent grew black.

"You can back out Holly, you know. We won't think you're a wimp," said T, popping up and down on her air mattress every time she moved.

"I'm fine," I said, gripping my flashlight. "This is great." Crickets were chirping, owls sang their summery song. Sie rolled on her squawking cot. Its metal springs squealed like an angry pig.

"I never camped out before, this is a first," T said, her mattress flopping around like a dolphin out of water as she turned toward me.

"It'll be a Wild adventure, Team," I said, then added, "we *are* only 30 feet from the house."

"Yeah, you're right," said Sie as she rolled over, her cot screeching like a scared rabbit. "Maybe we should get a radio to listen for the weather. We don't want storms creeping up on us in the dark."

"Maybe I should go to the bathroom one more time," said T. "But I don't want to go alone," she whined to her sister.

"Alright," said Sie, unzipping her bag. "Let's go. I'm right behind you."

"Don't forget to zip the door," I reminded them. "We don't want mosquitoes in here." They ran out of the tent and in the back porch door. In mere minutes they were back onto the wailing cot and flopping mattress.

"One bed was too soft, one was too hard and the other was just right," I said, as the cot squealed and the mattress bellowed as the two rolled about. "You know, from the Three B—um, never mind."

Sierra blinded me with her headlamp. She was trying to get the radio to work but the batteries were fused together.

"You could land airplanes with that beam. Isn't there another setting other than blinding?" I asked. She was clicking through different settings on the headlamp when T slid something out from under her cot.

"I'm kinda hungry again," T said, opening a cooler.

"What? Holey creeps!" I shot upright "You can't bring food

in here, it'll attract animals!"

"But I want a cheese stick," she said.

"Have your cheese stick while you take the cooler back into the house, T," ordered Sie. "We don't want unexpected guests, like rats or skunks."

"But I don't want to go alone," she whined.

"Fine, I'll go with you. I need Kleenex anyway. My allergies are acting up," Sie said, sniffing. She clicked on her headlamp and it blazed a light trail for them to follow to the house. The yard was lit up like a stadium as they raced to the porch door.

"Team work," I sighed and rolled over. The sooner I go to sleep the sooner morning will get here. It was going to be a long night with the girls getting up to go in the house every ten minutes. I puffed up my hoodie pillow and lay in the dark waiting for their return.

The Team was fast destroying any sense of wild camping I hoped to experience.

TAGTEAM, TEAMWORK

As the air got chilly on my sunburn, I slid on my hoodie, which had been my pillow. With nothing to rest my sunburned swollen alien head on, I clicked on my flashlight and found one of T's sweatshirts and rolled it up—much better!

It hadn't been two minutes when I heard the girls come back through the yard, barreling for the safety of the tent. They hit the tent door so hard it shook the whole thing and my flashlight bounced away in the dark.

"Holy creeps, guys, cool it," I said. "Remember this is Aunt Kitty's tent." I rearranged and fluffed up my new sweatshirt pillow. "And don't forget to zip up the door—no mosquitoes

inside, right?"

Annoyed at the Team's camping antics, I hoped this was their last trip of the night. There was sniffling and the zipper clinked near my head. Then the zipper slid up and the two tumbled into the tent, tripping over my boots as they came through the door. Sie was sniffling and T still smacking her lips when they climbed over the squeaking, squawking cot and onto the trampoline air mattress. Whoa did they smell bad! I wondered what kind of cheese T had eaten.

"I hope you had something that will hold you through the night. No more food runs or bathroom breaks. Good night. And zip the door shut!" Now I was so annoyed by the Team's behavior I forgot all about facing my fear of the dark. I just wanted to sleep. Then a mosquito bit my cheek, right on my favorite freckle. That was the last straw.

"Guys, I told you to zip up the tent!" I said angrily, sitting up. As I crawled to the door, I was blinded by the light beam of what must have been a semi-truck or incoming spaceship bouncing across the yard toward the tent.

"Guys?" I said, suddenly uncertain of what was happening. The girls grunted and whined. As I was putting on my boots they both leapt on me and we all tumbled in a stinky heap tripping on clothes and the wheezing mattress.

"Holly!! What's going on?" T called from outside the tent. Outside the tent?!? If that was Sie's light and T hollering out there, then who or what was in the tent with me?!? I rolled to the door as one intruder grabbed my bootlace and the other my hoodie string. The tent door flapped open and there stood T and Sie, with Gram and Aunt Kitty coming up behind.

There, in the light of Sie's headlamp were two sniffing,

slurping grunting young bear cubs! They tussled and fought over my boots and hoodie pockets which were covered in the raspberry jello from my log sturgeon. The hungry cubs were all over any place that had spilled jello on it.

"Holy creeps, times two!" yelped Sie and T in unison.

"Holly!" gasped Gram. "What are you doing?"

"Remain calm," ordered Aunt Kitty. The stench from the cubs was pretty bad and they were pretty strong. I was glad that they seemed to like me—or at least raspberry jello.

"If they're here, then w-where's their mother?" I asked

quietly. The group outside the tent suddenly got nervous and looked around. Then the girls bolted for the farmhouse.

"Good question, Holly," said Gram. Aunt Kitty was on the phone to Ranger Pearl as the two babies licked my hands and neck. They were pretty cute, but I really wanted to get out of the tent.

"Get up slowly, Holly," instructed Gram. The curious babies followed my every move and my jello soaked boots and hoodie. I walked out of the tent with the two clambering after me.

"Take them to the garage," said Aunt Kitty. We walked over while Gram opened the door. Once the cubs caught a whiff of a raspberry jello spill on the floor they were all over it with tongue and claw. We shut them in the garage.

"Holy creeps," I said leaning against the door. Gram and Aunt Kitty were bent over laughing.

"It's your red jello paint they wanted!" hooted Gram. Inside the garage the cubs were squalling and tussling in the dark.

Then things got quiet again.

"We'll wait inside the house until Pearl gets here. We really don't know when Mama Bear will show up. But for now they're safe," said Aunt Kitty. The twins watched from the back porch. Hunter was slobbering up the window with excitement. When I walked inside he went crazy from the bear cub stink all over me. The twins, wrapped in blankets, stared at me, then we all bust out laughing.

"I danced with bears!" I said. "It happened so fast I never had a moment to think about it or be afraid. I don't even care if I smell like a bear. I had my Wild bear moment, times two!"

"Which is why you're heading for the shower right now!" chuckled Gram, plugging her nose. "With your clothes on."

After my shower the twins and I were eating ice cream when Ranger Pearl and the Park Service arrived. We stepped outside into the moonlit night to watch the truck back up with a cage in the truck bed.

"I hear you had close encounters of the furred kind!" Ranger Pearl quipped and snorted at her joke, hooking her thumbs into her belt. The park workers opened the truck gate. They transferred the two wiggly cubs into a cage by using doughnuts and cookies.

"What's going to happen to them?" I asked Ranger Pearl.

"They'll be taken to a nearby rehabilitator and fed," she said. "Then we'll do a search for their mother. She has to be somewhere."

"Wow, the Sleeping Bear Legend in reverse," I said. "These cubs are hanging around waiting for their mother to show up."

"They must be pretty hungry," said one of the workers as he slammed the truck gate. "Because this is all that is left of some hunk of firewood that was in the garage. It smells like strawberries." He grimaced and held up a slime-coated bit of log. "They had a real picnic in there. Paper plates and all."

140

"Holy creeps! My log sturgeon!" I said, holding the chunk of pink wood. Gram and Aunt Kitty covered their mouths to stifle a laugh. "My log sturgeon for the art show tomorrow is gone."

"No wonder I couldn't find my jello to make my salad for tomorrow," giggled Aunt Kitty.

"Your log saved those cub's lives," said Ranger Pearl. "It brought them here out of harm's way. They could have been hit by a car or gotten killed by a larger predator."

"And because of your sloppy paint job, they had a good time, too," said Sie. "A *real* teddy bear picnic."

"Maybe this is what your dream bear wanted you to find all along—the cubs and their mother," said T, yawning.

"My Wild camp out tonight is cancelled," I said. I felt like T's deflated air mattress that had gotten a bear claw pushed through it. "The tent needs to be destinked and cleaned out."

"You'll get another chance to use it," said Gram, as she shuffled us off to bed. "Tomorrow is another day, and a big one at that."

No claw-tifact. No log sturgeon. No camp out. But I did dance with bears. I was more than ready for a good night's sleep, times ten.

141

TEDDY BEAR PICNIC TROUBLES

I woke up feeling creepy. I should have felt good knowing that I saved the cubs, but instead I felt all sick inside like a big, gooey, hairy, grumpy gummy bear gone sour.

"Since we've gotten here I've had night-bear nightmares, got scratched up, sunburned up, blistered, battered, and been in the same room as Ivy Buckthorn," I groaned. "I lost my good luck claw-tifact, didn't get my life-changing camp out and now—now my awesome log sturgeon is gone and will not be a hit."

"Well, it was a hit with the bear cubs," laughed Sie. "They really liked it a lot."

"We have been here for one whole week and we still haven't figured out the problem with the water," I sighed heavily. "I mean its cool and all that the cubs are safe but the lake is still losing water and we don't know why." The twins were quiet for a minute.

"But, I bet you're happy that your bad bear dreams are gone," said T, rolling out of bed. "They *are*, aren't they?"

"No, actually," I said. "The hairy gummy bear band was doing their "Teddy Bear Picnic" song and dance number again, only weirder." I scruffled my hair. My head felt better—a lot less alien-like.

"How can your dreams possibly be any more weird than they are now, Holly?" laughed Sie, sliding on her glasses.

"They're more annoying than frightening," I said. "They have eight-legs and look like hairy birthday balloons floating around, in all different colors and sizes."

Night-Bear Nightmare Bear Hugs!

"OK that is weird," sighed T, "but it's like a puzzle."

"I know, that's why my brain is boiling," I said. "I can't figure it out. I'll see what Bernie thinks," I said, pulling on my hat over my serious late shower bed head hair. The twins tried to stifle giggles.

"Geez you guys," I rolled my eyes. "We're going over to his house to pick up him up for the beach party trash art contest. Besides, I can use all the help I can get on this." I threw my sock at them to make them stop snickering.

When we got to Ranger Pearl's house she was on her way out the door. I think she lived in her uniform, belt and all.

"Glad you're here, troops," she said saluting us. "On my way to HQ. We found the sow—the mother bear—holed up under a shed in a peach orchard almost directly across from the Crouch Farm where you're staying. She's pretty messed up and weak from a run-in with a car. But she should be fine. We have her sedated so she's sleeping now. Those cubs were lucky. They've been foraging on their own for days and went out looking for fast food."

"Poor mom," said Sie.

"Poor cubs," said T.

"Where will they go?" I asked her.

"Not to worry, young lady. Mom and cubs will soon be on their way to a bear ranch in the U.P. where they'll be taken care of." Ranger Pearl drove off as Bernie came out.

"You kids hang out while I go get us some snacks from the store. I'll be back in a heartbeat," said Gram. Bernie had his swan art in a box.

"Sounds like you had an exciting night," he said, taking us to his room. "I'm glad you didn't meet the cub's mother. Come on, I made you something," he said to me.

"How's Fluffy doing?" I asked, peering into the tanks.

"A lot better with clean water." Fluffy did look happier as she swam around. She had a spark in her eye as T fed her a pinch of food.

144

Bernie held out a small leather pouch with a long leather drawstring. "In honor of your camp out, to hold your bear claw rock." He beamed. He had beaded a bear track on it.

"Thanks, Bernie. It's really cool," I said. "But remember, I lost my rock *and* I didn't get to camp out all night."

"I know," he said. "But maybe the rock will come back to you some day. And I'm sure you'll go on another camping trip. Nothing stops us Guardians and GeEKS from exploring." I smiled. He was right. I would have more adventures and I would always remember this Sleeping Bear adventure.

"Tell him your dream Holly," said T nudging me.

"It's the floating bears again," I said. "They look like puffy aliens with eight legs. They don't have teeth, but have walrus moustaches. They were singing 'Beware the teddy bear picnic!' over and over— all bubbly like they were under water."

"The Barber Shop Water Bear Quartet," joked Sie. Then Bernie snapped his fingers and pulled a book down from his shelf. He quickly flipped through the pages.

"Dig it!" he beamed. "Did they look like this?" He stuck the book in my face.

"Holy creeps! Yes!" The girls gathered around the book.

"It's no alien or invasive specie. It's a native creature that lives in the water. It's a 'water bear', or Tardigrades. It means 'slow walker'. There," he said, pointing at the picture.

"Tardy what?" asked T.

"Tardigrades," I said. "Sounds like a name Ivy would call someone in school."

"They live in the sand. And mosses and lichens as well as in the water," Bernie read.

"It's the squishy gummy bear I've dreamed about since the first night we got here," I said and slapped my sore red forehead. "They're warning me about the picnic today. Something about the water."

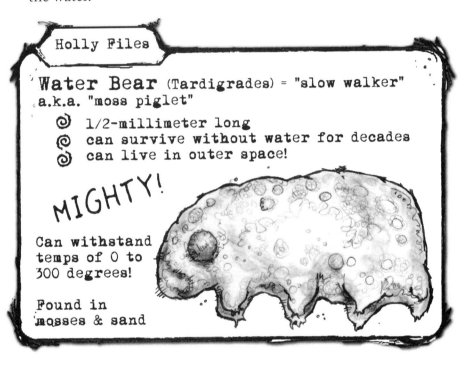

Holly Files

Water Bear (Tardigrades) = "slow walker" a.k.a. "moss piglet"

- 1/2-millimeter long
- can survive without water for decades
- can live in outer space!

MIGHTY!

Can withstand temps of 0 to 300 degrees!

Found in mosses & sand

"The Three Bears and Goldilock's cottage!" T exclaimed. "Maybe there really is something going on in Buckthorn's shed!"

"Remember the sign with the bad spelling?" said Sie. "Never trust anyone with spelling that bad." Then all of our eyes met.

"Holy creeps! I forgot all about this! I found it next to Buckthorn's shed!" I said, digging into my pocket and pulling out the crumpled paper litter I had found in the ferns two days before. I opened the paper and smoothed it out. "'Buckthorn Brew—Icy Dunes—Glacier Spring Water'," I read aloud. We all looked at each other again.

"It's in the water! In Buckthorn's shed!" I exclaimed. "I thought the bottles in the shed were waiting to be recycled but I bet the label was printed to go *on* the bottles!"

"And Ivy said yesterday she was going to be Miss Buckthorn Brew and that there was going to be a big surprise!" Sie said. "I'll be they're selling bottled water today at the beach party to make lots of money!"

"They must be pumping it out of the lake and bottling it in the shed!" Bernie cried. "We gotta stop them! We gotta check that water!"

"Gross," said T.

"Gross is right. If they're not doing it right it'll make people super sick," said Bernie, calling his aunt. I gave him the label from the bottle. As Gram was coming in the door we pushed her back out.

"What in the world, kids?" said Gram as we pulled her to the van.

"We'll tell you on the way," I said. "We have to get to that picnic—fast!"

We told Aunt Kitty and Gram what we suspected on the way to the beach.

WATERSHED AND WATERBEARS

Aunt Kitty called Ranger Pearl from the car and told her to get over to the Buckthorn cottage at Bass Lake to check out our hunch.

"This is scary business, kids," whistled Gram. "If the bottled water is contaminated, people could get *very* sick."

Luckily, it was still early and only a few beach-goers had shown up. As we climbed out of the van we spotted a girl sitting atop a giant water bottle float.

"What in the world is *that*," said Sie, pointing. We all stood with our mouths hanging open. Then I realized the *that* was— Ivy Buckthorn.

Buckthorn Brew
Organic, fat-free spring water

"Miss Buckthorn Brew", as the sash around her shoulder read, was holding a bottle of water over her head and talking like a woman on an infomercial.

"Everyone needs water right?" she bellowed. "And everyone buys water, fancy glacier water stuff from Detroit and spring water from France. But Buckthorn's Beach Brew is both, spring water and glacier water. This here's the 'Icy Dunes 10 oz. Traveler's Spring Water'. Stick it in your fanny pack or down your mother's back. Organic, fat-free and natural. A mineral packed diet aid. A homegrown fresh and tasty swill. Chug a lug of Buckthorns."

The whole bunch of us Guardians ran up to Ivy. This time the entire team and I were flailing our arms wildly like crazy people to get her attention.

"Ivy! Drop that bottle!" I hollered.

"Squirrelberry! Freaks! What gives?" she sneered in her costume, holding the bottle high.

"Have you sold any yet, Ivy?" asked Gram.

"What's it to ya?" she scowled. Then she sighed and hung her head. "I'm sure we'll make lots of sales later when the kids arrive. Kids are always thirsty."

"So is that a no?" I asked.

"Yes, it's a no. I haven't sold any yet," she glared at me. "Daddy has the change. He doesn't trust me with it. He said to wait 'til he got back so I've been sitting here waiting." We all sighed with relief.

"Good, maybe Pearl can get to the cottage in time to stop him," said Gram, catching her breath.

"Oh, Daddy's not in his Water Shed at the cottage," Ivy said squinting at us. "My daddy is over there in that port-a-john. He's been in there for like an hour now. And frankly, I'm getting tired of sitting up here."

"I'll go find Mr. Buckthorn," said Aunt Kitty, hustling over

to where people had gathered around the green portable restroom.

"So where's the water, dear? The bottles of water?" asked Gram.

"Right here. He loaded up a bunch this morning."

Behind her was a blue-tarped mountain of glacial dune swill. Ivy unscrewed the cap of the bottle she held.

"Holy creeps! Stop!" I cried. "Don't drink that water, Ivy!"

"Huh?" she looked at the bottle in her hand. "How do I know if you're not tricking me? You just don't want my daddy to get rich."

"What she is saying, Ivy," explained Gram, "is that Ranger Pearl has to test the water first to see if it's drinkable." Right then the port-a-john crowd gasped and scattered. Aunt Kitty came running.

"Ivy there's something wrong with your father," Aunt Kitty said, looking worried. "Is your mother nearby? We have to get him to a hospital. It appears that he has gotten a taste of his own organic water."

"Um, she's over in the shade tent where the food is set up. She's not feeling well. She's pregnant, you know." Gram ran to get Mrs. Buckthorn.

Ranger Pearl appeared with more Park Rangers. In one hand she held a bullhorn and the other she pointed at the boxes of Buckthorn Brew.

"Gasping gobies!" the bullhorn crackled. "Shut that booth down before one bottle gets sold!" People froze in their tracks. "Where is Mr. Buckthorn?" Ranger Pearl belted.

"In the port-a-john," answered Aunt Kitty. Ivy slid off of her

plastic perch and we followed them to the row of portable potties. "He's been locked inside all morning."

"I'll just bet he is! None of his water has been purified or filtered," said Ranger Pearl. "If anyone drinks the water, they'll have giardia." The crowd surrounding the green plastic building gasped.

"What is giardia?" Mrs. Buckthorn asked weakly.

"Um, bad news in the bathroom department," said Gram. "Diarrhea for days."

"But the water is clean—straight from the lake. He's been pumping it in his Water Shed to make more money with the baby coming," Mrs. Buckthorn said, patting her belly. "He said it was spring water, because he started gathering it in March."

"Holy giardia, times ten!" gasped Gram, sitting Mrs. Buckthorn down.

"We just got back from his 'watershed'," Ranger Pearl made quote fingers in the air. "We saw no filtering system anywhere."

"He's been in the bathroom at least five times today," said Mrs. Buckthorn. "Poor Alder, will he be alright?"

Lights from an ambulance flashed as it worked its way through the growing crowd. Paramedics jumped out and tried talking a moaning Buckthorn out of the port-a-john. He finally emerged holding his paisley clad belly. The crowd took three big steps back and held their noses.

"Mr. Buckthorn," said Ranger Pearl, "do you know what a water cycle is?"

"A two-wheeled vehicle you ride to the beach?" The crowd all moaned.

"That's what I thought," said Pearl. "Get this man to a hospital." The paramedics strapped Mr. Buckthorn onto the waiting gurney.

"I was just trying to make a buck," he said. "I read about these guys getting filthy rich off spring water. Oooh, I'm not feeling so good!" He belched and moaned as he was loaded into the emergency vehicle.

"Hey, girlie," a little kid yanked on Ivy's sparkly sash and pointed at her water bottle. "That water has sea monkeys in it."

WATER, GOOD AND BAD

Mrs. Buckthorn climbed into the waiting ambulance while Ivy looked on with us. "Hurry, Ivy, get in, we have to go," Mrs. Buckthorn motioned to her. Ivy dropped her water bottle in the sand and looked paler than usual. Her father moaned and belched. Ivy stood speechless—probably for the first time ever in her life.

"Ivy, dear," said Aunt Kitty, half pushing Ivy inside the ambulance. "Your parents need you. Best of luck, Buckthorns!" And with that, the paramedic shut the door and the vehicle rolled away.

"Whew, that'll be a long ride," said Gram. "For all of them." The Team and I groaned. A park worker replaced the sloppy, incorrectly spelled 'CLOSED OUT OF ODER' sign on the port-a-john with something more official-looking as we went to unload our trash art.

"Ivy was right," I said. "She did say that they would become famous today. No one will ever forget this." Everyone laughed and stayed clear of the rank restroom.

"We all need water, clothing, food and shelter," said Aunt Kitty. "It's using what we have wisely and protecting it for others that come down the trail that's important. That and knowing as much as we can about our world and how it works."

"In Mr. Buckthorn's case, knowing more about water would've been a good thing," said Gram.

"What are we going to do with all of this water," asked Sie. "Sand castle party?"

"Nope. We'll dump it back in the lake," I said, "Where it came from." Ranger Pearl was already on that. Volunteers and families gathered to help load the water into waiting green Park Service pickup trucks.

"We'll have a water release party!" I said.

"I'll bet Misha-Makwa's happy now," T said, taking a swig from her own metal water bottle, filled from the tap at the farm house. Gram offered to stay behind and set-up the art exhibit while we all followed the Park trucks to release the water.

Once at Bass Lake, families lined the shore and poured in water as children held open bags to recycle the bottles. In no time we had dumped in most of what Mr. Buckthorn had pumped out.

When we got back to the Sleeping Bear P.A.W. picnic and art show, people were gathered around Ivy's twisted turtle poster and T's loon poster. They were a big hit. The good, the bad *and* the ugly had made an impression on people.

Families enjoyed the art show and really got into the sand sculpting. The Team and I made awesome sand sculptures and placed trash-art ducks and shorebirds on the beach to stand watch over them. Bernie's trumpeter swan came in first for trash art and was taken to the Visitor's Center to be put on display. Ranger Pearl gave us each a T-shirt for all of the hard work we'd done.

"Case closed," said Sie as we collapsed back at the farmhouse kitchen table.

"I want to remember this forever," said T.

"I will," I said. "I need a vacation after this vacation! And I don't think I'll ever eat another gummy bear for as long as I live. Or at least until next week."

"We should make a big thank you card for the park for letting us stay here and help," said Sie.

"Good idea, Sie," I said. "Make it a giant postcard about everything we did here."

"Maybe they'll put it up in the Visitor Center so everyone can see it all year long," said Bernie. T ran for supplies. The Team was in action once again.

We cut out T's drawing of Misha-Makwa and her cubs. Bernie drew a sturgeon and a swan feather. I painted a watery background. Sie made a map of the park. Then T tore out notes and bits of the Sleeping Bear legend from our notebook and we glued it all on a board. And for the finishing touch, like frosting on a cake, I glued some sand from my boot onto the map for the park shoreline.

"There! It tells the whole story of our park visit and what we

found here," I said proudly, calling Gram and Aunt Kitty in to see. I only wished it could have included everything we'd found and seen.

"Now that's teamwork!" said Gram.

Ranger Pearl stopped by to pick up Bernie and to say goodbye to us. It had been a long day, a long week, a long vacation.

"So Holly, tell me about the artifact you found," said Gram, serving Ranger Pearl lemonade. I sighed.

"Well, it was a pinkish stone," I said. "It really looked like a bear claw. I couldn't tell if it was a fossil or an artifact. But it was cool." Gram looked at Aunt Kitty. Ranger Pearl unsnapped one of the cool pouches on her belt.

"Did it look like this?" she asked, laying it on the table.

"My claw-tifact!" I yelped. Even though I don't need it for good luck, or to keep away bears or to help me face my fears anymore, I still missed it. And I want to use it as a tool in my exploring kit until I do get a real knife. Someday Mom says I can have a real knife, like when I learn to walk without falling. That might be a really long time, so until then this would do.

"I found it on the trail when we picked up the golf cart with the flat," Ranger Pearl said, hooking her thumbs into her belt. "It will be a good reminder of everything that happened here."

The stone fit perfectly in the bag Bernie made me. I tied it to my belt to have my own leather pouch like Ranger Pearl had.

"Thank you, Ranger Pearl," I said. "Oh! I almost forgot! We all made a big card for the Park to thank you for having us here." Sie and T brought in the big poster board art. Ranger Pearl studied it and nodded her head, then wiped her eyes.

"You Wilds make a pretty darned good GeEK team," she said to Aunt Kitty, and polished her glasses.

"The more the merrier!" I said. "With Guardians and GeEKs working together we can make a difference."

WATERS UNDER THE BRIDGE

"Speaking of making a difference, what's on the agenda for the rest of the summer?" Gram asked Aunt Kitty.

"I'm not quite sure what will happen now," Aunt Kitty said. "Go home, I guess. Give Hunter a bath. Relax."

It had been an amazing couple of weeks. I missed Kenny, Boy, Mom and Dad. I'm sure the team missed their families too. Hayfields could not have been the same without us. Just then Hunter began scratching at the door.

"I don't think he liked the bath part. He's trying to escape," said T.

Aunt Kitty giggled. "He's been sniffing and smelling every corner and crevice of the front porch," she said.

"Hope there are aren't any more bears out there," laughed Sie, shoving me playfully.

"Oh, I just remembered!" said Ranger Pearl. "An envelope for all of you arrived at the park office today. With all of the chaos I forgot to give it to you." She went to her truck and brought it in. Aunt Kitty sat at the kitchen table and opened it. Inside where postcards and sealed letters for each of us. Hunter barked and whined by the door.

"Could you girls take Hunter out and see what he needs?" Gram asked us.

"Sure," I said. "Let's go Team." The four of us took Hunter into the front yard. He sniffed around the porch, where he had really done a number on the wood. He pulled Bernie to a tall tree by the road.

"What is it, boy?" Bernie asked. Something above us rustled in the leaves and made a small grunting noise. Hunter whined and quivered. Over our heads in the tree sat a porcupine, all silvery with a chocolate brown face. Bernie immediately took Hunter back into the house. Dogs and porcupines do not mix, and when they do, it's painful for both. Bernie ran back out to where we stood.

"Aha! I'll bet you're the one who ate the porch steps, not Hunter," he said.

"Gram used to tell me tales about porcupines eating off the ax handles in Pauline's lumber camp," I said. "They're looking for salt from sweaty hands."

"Dig it," said Bernie, looking up at it with me. "They are so cool—and cute." The porcupine shifted, its quills clacking and settling, to get a better look at us. The twins giggled.

"Hey Mr. Prickly Butt," I said. "What do you have to say?"

"Come on, Holly, we should leave it alone," said T, backing towards the house.

"Wait a minute. The porky is talking to me."

"Holly," Sie rolled her eyes. "Not again. Enough with the animal messengers already."

"It's fun talking to animals," I said as I waved goodbye to the porcupine. When we got back inside Gram was at the table, holding a bunch of letters and postcards. She smiled as she handed us each something to read from home.

"This is cool, like we are away at camp or something," I said. "This is a postcard for me from Boy. 'Making music and money cutting grass.' He says he will feed Kenny next week—if we don't come home. Hmm, I wonder what he means by *if*." I looked at Gram.

Aunt Kitty took her turn. "I've been invited to visit a friend of mine in the U.P., Woody Timberlake. He works at a park at the west side of the state." We turned to Sie and T as they read over their letter together. A crayon drawing by Savannah covered most of the envelope it came in.

"Wow," cried T. "This is amazing!"

"What?" I asked.

"I can't believe this," Sie looked up at me and lay the letter down. "Our mom won an Artist-In-Residence competition! It's in the U.P.—in the Porcupine Mountain State Wilderness Area. She gets to stay in a cabin there for two weeks and make art!" Both of their eyes were wide.

"That's wonderful, Miss Sierra, and quite a coincidence," grinned Aunt Kitty. "That's where I'm headed, also."

"We're all packing for the Porcupines!" I leaped up. Hunter bayed. "I told you the Porcupines were calling me. It's a Wild thing." I looked at the girls and shrugged. I think they were starting to believe that we Wild women are kind of weird and kind of special all at the same time.

"There's always more to explore," I said. "It takes a Team to raise a village—or something."

With that Ranger Pearl and Bernie said their goodbyes. We were official Guardians and Bernie an official GeEK. He was our Great Lakes, Sleeping Bear HQ connection.

Aunt Kitty decided for our last night at Sleeping Bear Dunes we would all go up to Empire Bluffs to watch the sun set. Walking along the overlook I gazed out over Lake Michigan. So much water. Bernie had a big job ahead of him, trying to protect this. We all did.

We sat on the benches as the sun went down, thinking about all that had happened and what new adventures awaited us. As if reading my mind, Gram said, "The Porkies, as the locals call the Porcupine Mountains, is almost a nine hour drive from here. As far west as you can get and still be in Michigan!"

"Now *that* is wilderness," said Sie whistling.

"Wow. The land of my Wild relatives, home to wilderness and wild things," I said. I thought about the porcupine in the tree. "Sie, remember when you said you were waiting for Piglet to arrive and take me to the One Hundred Acre Wood? It looks

Empire Bluffs

like he did just that, in the tree outside the farmhouse."

The evening sky was all purple and pink over Lake Michigan. In the distance were the cubs of legend, the Manitou Islands—North and South. High above the beach, on top of the tallest dune, lie their mother, the ghost bear, Misha-Makwa, watching over them.

"*Now* she's sleeping. And tonight, so will I!" I said. "I'll miss this place—and Bernie." I added. The girls smiled.

"He's a pretty cool lake guardian dude," said Sie. I hooked my thumbs into my belt and smiled. We said our goodbyes to the lake and dunes.

"To the Porkies, Team!" I said. "I wonder what that place is like." I imagined porcupines walking the mountains at midnight under the full moon. I patted my bear claw-tifact in its new pouch.

"Something about the name 'wilderness' makes me wiggly," said T.

"Wilderness is just an undeveloped and protected zone used by wild species," said Aunt Kitty. "A place that has not been significantly modified by human activity—no roads, pipelines and other structures. Our wilderness areas are some of the last wild places left on earth."

"Last wild place left on earth?!" I said. "Team Wild, let's go!"

Lori Taylor *is a Michigan artist/author/illustrator who has wandered the state's woods and waters on foot, bike, kayak or canoe for stories ever since she was a child. She teaches kids to "poke the world with a stick" to get to know nature. Lori lives among varied reptiles, mammals, and birds on five acres in Pinckney, MI , home of Bear Track Press. When Lori is not reading, writing, drawing, kayaking, hiking, or camping in the wild—she is playing with her grandkids!*

To see more of Lori's art, books, photos, and fun Holly WIld FREEBIE stuff, visit:

www.loritaylorart.com

Pierce Stocking Drive

For lotsa cool stuff on the
Sleeping Bear Dunes National Lakeshore:

http://www.nps.gov/slbe/index.htm
Visit: Philip A. Hart Visitor Center
Empire, MI

Also, a place where **YOU** can dance with
baby bears, learn about and feed them is:

Oswald's Bear Ranch
http://www.oswaldsbearranch.com/
Newberry, MI

167

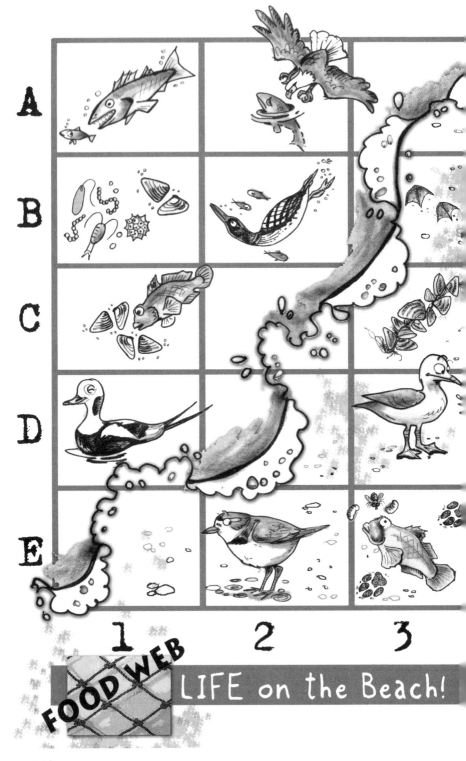

A

B

C

D

E

1 2 3

FOOD WEB

LIFE on the Beach!

168

4   **5**   **6**

"When one tugs at a single thing in nature,
he finds it attached to the rest of the world!"

John Muir

LIFE ON THE BEACH!

Beachcomb the *"food web"* (pages 168 and 169) to find the answers

1. _____ Food chain! Big eat little. That's nature's way.
2. _____ Trash-eating animal.
3. _____ Who ate an inflatable party favor? _____
4. _____ Interdunal Pond.
5. _____ Noisy, feathered scavenger.
6. _____ Ghost forest. Boo!
7. _____ Bacteria-packed Round goby food.
8. _____ Forest edge predator. *HINT: "Perfect-step" tracks.*
9. _____ Endangered shorebird larvae-eater.
10. _____ Chain of deadly "aliens".
11. _____ Plankton. *HINT: Tiny fish food.*
12. _____ Who got tangled up in a lure? _____
13. _____ Forested back dune.
14. _____ Who needs to be on a leash? _____
15. _____ Diving bird eats fish. *HINT: They are NOT ducks!*
16. _____ Feathered zebra mussel-eater.
17. _____ Forgotten picnics spell T-R-O-U-B-L-E!
18. _____ Endangered chicks need protecting!
19. _____ Who got into poision ivy and can give it to humans?
    HINT: "Sloppy walker" tracks. _____
20. _____ Hog-nosed predator.
21. _____ Who gets sick from eating dead goby? _____
22. _____ Flying raptor eats sick fish. Top o' the food chain can be
    trouble time 3!

"What's
in YOUR
lake water?"

__water boatman
__fairy shrimp
__water flea
__rotifers
__algae
__?

Grab a magnifier and look at lake water!
Draw what you see. Count how many things you see.

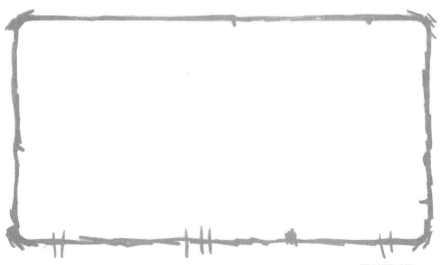

BERNIE'S BEACHCOMBING NOTES:

- Learn more about our lakes and water and what lives in them.

- **Take back the TAP!** Drink your H20 from glass or metal bottles.

- The BREAKDOWN on breaking down—decomposing!

🌀 **Lake Sturgeon** (Acipenser fulvescens) **a.k.a. Nme'(nah-MAY)**

Dates back to the time of the dinosaurs. (A PREHISTORIC SURVIVOR!!!)
Lives: 50 - 150 years old.
Description: 5 rows of sharp "scutes", torpedo-shaped.
Bottom-dweller in deep lakes, streams.
Legally protected--THREATENED SPECIES!!!
State Status: IMPERILED!!!

glurp!

"barbels"
smell food: leeches, larva,
crayfish, small fish

"scutes", bony plates with
hooked spurs protect young
from predators. YUCKY!

🌀 **THREATS to NME':**
Nme' are on the decline worldwide from: habitat loss, loss of
nursery area, spawning grounds, pollution, invasive species,
lack of food, industry, depleted habitats.

WHEW! "Help Me!" says Nahme.

TOP 10 FINDS OF HUMAN "INVASIVE" KINDS

(and how many **YEARS** it takes for each to **BREAKDOWN**:)

1. **cigarette butt 1.5—10**
2. **caps/lids 75**
3. **food wrapper/containers (styrofoam) 500**
4. **drinking straws 700**
5. **cigar tips 25**
6. **plastic bags 500—1,000**
7. **cups/plates/utensils 7—100 (longer if buried)**
8. **plastic bottles 450**
9. **glass bottles 1,000—1 million**
10. **beverage cans 50—200**

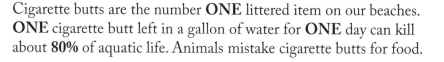

Cigarette butts are the number **ONE** littered item on our beaches.
ONE cigarette butt left in a gallon of water for **ONE** day can kill
about **80%** of aquatic life. Animals mistake cigarette butts for food.

KICK SOME BUTTS!

TWIN-POWER, TEAM POWER!

What to do with all of those plastic bottles?

Bernie has great ideas and everyone loves to make things!
Try making TRASH art, TRASH games and TRASH tools!

Try TRASH CRAFTS!

BeACh in a BOttLE

Add small things:

stones, glitter

beads, buttons

rice

Fill empty bottle with rice

tack, screw

nuts, seeds

money, shells

Keep a list of what you hid in the bottle. See if your friend can find all the items. WHAT is YOUR beach hiding? Which item will decompose first? Which won't?

WATER CyCLE GarDen

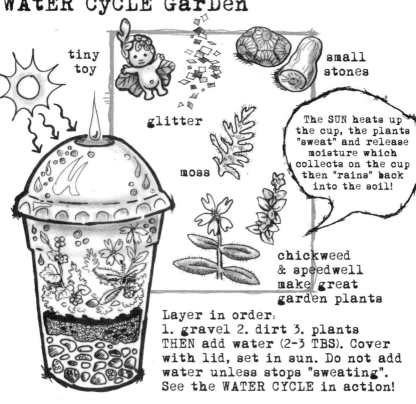

tiny
toy

glitter

moss

small
stones

The SUN heats up
the cup, the plants
"sweat" and release
moisture which
collects on the cup
then "rains" back
into the soil!

chickweed
& speedwell
make great
garden plants

Layer in order:
1. gravel 2. dirt 3. plants
THEN add water (2-3 TBS). Cover
with lid, set in sun. Do not add
water unless stops "sweating".
See the WATER CYCLE in action!

clouds
cool,
water falls

plants
"sweat"
water

LAKE

WATER Cycle!

The HOLLY Pages!

BIG
fossil
"CLAW-TifAct"

6"
long

That's
longer than
this book
is wide!

Arctodus
simus claw

BE A GEEK! (GEO-EXPLORER KID)
Explore the outdoors! Find and draw your good luck charm below!

You met our smallest "bear" now, meet Michigan's BIGGEST BEAR!
Our largest land mammal predator.

Holly Files

◎ **Arctodus simus**
"bulldog or short-faced bear" was a running bear. It could run 30-40 m.p.h.

EXTINCT

◎ Stood 12' tall

◎ Died 12,500 years ago

Draw what you think its skull looked like!

POP-Bottle Fishing Kit

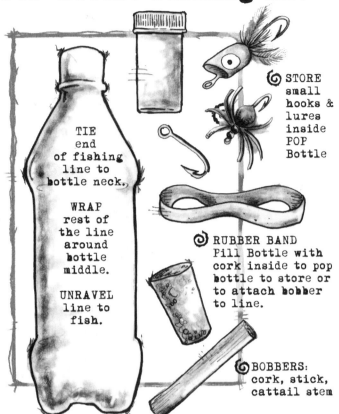

GO FISH!

TIE end of fishing line to bottle neck.

WRAP rest of the line around bottle middle.

UNRAVEL line to fish.

⊚ STORE small hooks & lures inside POP Bottle

⊚ RUBBER BAND Pill Bottle with cork inside to pop bottle to store or to attach bobber to line.

⊚ BOBBERS: cork, stick, cattail stem

Holly Files

BAiT
Catch live bait yourself!

⊚ Nightcrawlers come out at night after a rain.

⊚ Turn logs, rocks and damp leaves for juicy worms.

⊚ Catch crickets and grasshoppers with a small net.

178

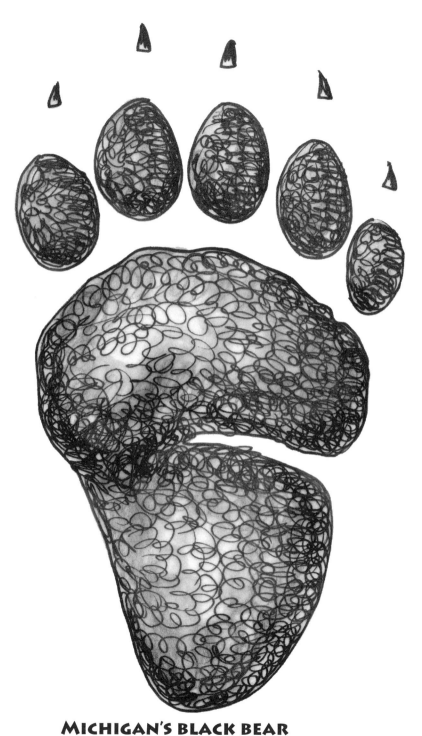

MICHIGAN'S BLACK BEAR
Actual size track. Place your hand on the page!